*A Rex Graves Mystery*

# MURDER

# ~ AT THE ~

# DOLPHIN INN

C. S. CHALLINOR

First Edition

Cover art © Can Stock Photo, Inc., 2012

Book cover, design, and production by Perfect Pages
Literary Management, Inc.

ISBN-13: 978-1475219906
ISBN-10: 1475219903

# PREVIOUS TITLES

# ACKNOWLEDGMENTS

My grateful thanks to Douglas P. Lyle, M.D., who conscientiously and courteously answered my medical questions for *Murder at the Dolphin Inn* and *Murder of the Bride*.

*The Dolphin Inn*

*Key West, FL*

#1, *McCullers Suite ~ Bill Reid*

#2, *Tennessee Williams Suite ~ Mae & Emily Hart*

#3, *Hemingway Suite ~ Diane S. Dyer*

#4, *Jimmy Buffet Suite ~ Dennis & Peggy Barber*

#5, *Robert Frost Suite ~ vacant*

#6, *Audubon Suite ~ Chuck & Alma Shumaker*

#7, *Writer's Garret ~ Michelle Cuzzens & Ryan Ford*

#8, *Poet's Attic ~ vacant*

~ONE~

Gift-wrapped in yellow ribbon, the Dolphin Inn stood amid a lush landscape abloom with orchids, red-spiked bromeliads, and Chinese Palm fans. White porches decorated with gingerbread trim wrapped long arms around the lilac clapboard, while a transom window depicting frolicking blue dolphins topped the Victorian mansion's front door. Hard to imagine a double homicide taking place here, Rex thought. The bed-and-breakfast was, to use a British expression, rather "twee."

Geckos skittered before his sandals on the brick path that led to a white picket fence separating the property from the street, where he had left his fiancée among a crowd of onlookers. Undeterred by the traffic cones, their number had increased in the half hour or so since he had been inside the guest house. There would doubtless have been more spectators had it not been the morning after the annual Fantasy Fest Parade, a night of heavy drinking and revelry, which he and Helen had missed as they sailed from Miami to Mallory Square on a Carnival cruise ship.

Empty beer cans and strings of iridescent beads littered the sun-dappled sidewalks of the street. Rex derived no small measure of satisfaction thinking that the fall weather back home in Scotland would be gray and drizzly; not balmy as here in Key West. Dressed for the most part in slogan T-shirts, shorts, and sunglasses, the rubberneckers formed an almost comical contrast to the dark-uniformed and serious-countenanced city cops on duty displaying the blue and gold patches of the KWPD on their sleeves.

"He really fancies himself, doesn't he?" Helen said, nodding in the direction of the patrol officer on guard outside the gate. His upper body was muscle-bound to the point of diminished mobility, and he wore a wide brimmed hat cocked jauntily on his head, his black holster polished to the patina of glass. "Is it true the two dead bodies are dressed up as clowns?" she asked.

"Aye," Rex replied in his Lowland Scots. He had just seen them. Hands bound, plastic bags over their heads, they sat slumped on the floor of the kitchen. "Merle and Taffy Dyer, owners of the bed-and-breakfast. Died of asphyxiation, it would appear."

"Who did you speak to?"

2

"Captain Dan Diaz, the ranking detective. Pleasant chap, but not verra forthcoming. As to be expected." Rex conceded the man had a lot on his hands.

"I was talking to someone called Mike, an innkeeper on Francis Street. Handsome devil. He was quite chatty," Helen added with a pleased smile.

"You mean he tried to chat you up."

"He told me the owners had been running the Dolphin Inn for six years, after selling their bed-and-breakfast in Vermont. She was an alcoholic, and her husband a controlling miser. Seems the son hated his parents with a vengeance. The daughter is recently divorced and brought her two whiny children to stay while she got back on her feet."

"This Mike knows a lot."

"He said the Key West Association of Innkeepers is a very tight-knit community."

"So it would seem."

Reporters gathered even as they watched. The double murder of two respectable citizens was big news. A pod of marked and unmarked vehicles nosing the curb offloaded EMS personnel, while two-way radios emitted a steady stream of flat-toned static. A wave of tension rippled through the crowd.

"Seems a bit ghoulish standing here waiting for the body bags to be carried out to the morgue,"

Helen remarked. "There's loads to see in Key West, and we only have a few hours before we have to get back on our ship."

"Och, we're not really going to get back on that floating monstrosity, are we?"

"What do you mean?" his fiancée asked, stiffening in her yellow sun dress.

"I mean, the cabin is stifling and I bumped my head getting out of bed this morning. Plus, our waiter looks and sounds like a poor imitation of Dracula. Where do they find these people?"

"He's Romanian."

"Transylvania used to be in Romania, didn't it?"

Helen tried to suppress a smile, and failed miserably. "So, what do you suggest, exactly?"

"Let's retrieve our luggage and stay in Key West."

"But what about Mexico?"

"What aboot it?"

"I wanted to sample some real margaritas."

"We can get margaritas here. Jimmy Buffet made Key West the Margaritaville of the world."

"But it's a free cruise," Helen insisted. She had won it in a sweepstakes on a previous cruise to the Caribbean.

"All the more reason to chuck it," Rex pointed out. He had only agreed to the cruise with great reluctance. "And the return voyage doesn't bear thinking aboot—two full days at sea watching hairy chest contests on deck." He couldn't imagine anything worse.

Helen's face dissolved into a mischievous grin. "I was going to enter you! Ah, well." She sighed in capitulation. "So what do we do now? Assuming we can get out of the cruise..."

"Find a place to stay."

Helen consulted her tourist map. "Mike's bed-and-breakfast is on Frances Street. He told me he's always fully booked in October, but he may be able to recommend somewhere."

"What aboot here?"

"What do you mean, Rex?" The tone in which she said "Rex" did not bode well for his plans.

"There's a vacancy. The innkeeper said he'd offer us a discount."

"I should think so," she exploded. "It's a murder scene!"

"Could have been a suicide pact," he said to placate her.

"You don't think that for a moment. I know you. You want to stay here so you can solve the murders. I cannot believe this!" She put her foot down, literally, stomping her sandaled foot on the pavement.

Rex gazed with regret at the lilac façade of the guest house. "You're right, lass. This was supposed to be a romantic trip. But the bodies are in a separate part of the house, and there's no blood or mess whatsoever." Just two shrink-wrapped heads. "It's squeaky clean," he assured her.

Helen shot him a sardonic look. "Surprising the police would let the guests stay, don't you think?" she remarked.

"Why not? Easier to keep an eye on everybody that way. And, as I said, the bodies are in an annex, closed off from the rest of the premises by a passageway."

"How can you be so nonchalant?"

"Just practical. And you'll like this: The suites are named after famous writers who lived or stayed in Key West. Hemingway, Tennessee Williams..." Rex, having forgotten the others, brandished the B & B brochure in his hand and looked at her hopefully.

The wind appeared to go out of her sails as she exhaled a deep breath. "What would we have to do to cancel our cruise?"

"The innkeepers' son said he would contact the cruise line. We simply retrieve our bags and let the *Fantasia* set sail without us. I'll go back in and see what he managed to arrange," Rex said before she could change her mind.

If they stayed, he might even get the chance to see his son again before they returned to the UK. Pursuing his studies in marine science in Jacksonville, Campbell had met up with his dad and Helen in Miami for an all too brief visit.

"I heard there's great shopping on Duval Street..." Helen held out her palm.

Grinning, Rex extracted his American Express card from his wallet, and she flicked it out of his fingers.

"Thank you!" she chirped. "Meet you back here at eleven."

Encircling her waist, he kissed her on the ear. "You're a great sport, Helen."

"So you keep telling me. I just hope I don't live to regret this."

# ~TWO~

What he had seen upon venturing into the Dolphin Inn kitchen prior to persuading Helen to stay were two inert clowns sitting side by side in front of the industrial size oven, tongues protruding rudely from big red lips, which resembled gashes in the white-powdered faces tinged with blue. Bloodshot eyes stared through clear plastic bags puckered beneath the chins and tied with thin yellow nylon rope.

Their garb consisted of matching black and white tops accessorized with plastic red bow ties of the spinning variety; black pants; candy-striped socks; and black patent pumps on feet splayed on the linoleum floor. A shoeprint lifting kit stood by the side door, though Rex had seen no visible prints from where he stood back from the scene.

He reflected that the lurid tableau, rendered extra garish beneath the fluorescent strip lighting, might have been more in keeping with Halloween than Fantasy Fest. That was before he discovered that the theme for this year's festival was "Halloween Pre-Scream."

"The innkeepers?" he had asked the Hispanic detective upon venturing into the kitchen.

An athletic man of five foot-ten in pressed khakis and a white polo shirt, the officer introduced himself as Captain Dan Diaz of the Key West Police Department. He referred to his small steno pad. "Merle and Taffy Dyer, sixty-five and sixty-three years old, originally from Vermont. Their son found them at seven this morning when he came in to make breakfast for the guests. He lives a short distance away."

Diaz got on his cell phone. "What's keeping you?" he demanded, and apparently receiving an unsatisfactory answer, uttered a short expletive as he snapped the phone shut.

"Any suspects yet?" Rex asked.

"Just about anyone you can think of. The Dyers weren't real popular."

"No sign of a struggle," Rex observed, looking around the orderly kitchen with its institutional stainless steel counters, as no doubt required by the board of health.

"And no pry marks on the exterior of the door to the alley. House keys were found on the bodies. Could be a suicide pact, but their hands are bound behind their backs. Just possible they could have tied each other's hands, but it's a stretch." Diaz smiled at his own choice of words.

"I'd say that was unlikely," Rex concurred. "They'd have had to put the bags on first, and before they got their hands tied, they would likely both have suffocated. And you'd think they would commit suicide in the privacy of their bedroom, not dressed in a silly disguise for all the staff and guests to see. And look." Rex stepped toward the bodies.

Detective Diaz held him back smartly. "This is a crime scene. Watch where you walk. In fact, you shouldn't be here in the first place, bubba."

Undeterred, Rex pointed. "That scuff mark on the lino? Looks like the bodies were dragged backwards from the door. That would explain why the bigger clown's shoe is off the heel."

"Possibly. But I must ask you to leave. Forensics will be here any minute. They got snagged in traffic. With the tourists leaving Key West after the parade, you got gridlock all around the island." Diaz consulted his pad again. "I know where to find you if I need to ask you anything else. What room did you say?"

"Ehm, I didn't," Rex admitted. "I'm no officially staying at the Dolphin," he said in his Scots accent. "Not yet, anyway. I saw the crime scene tape outside and thought I'd take a gander."

Detective Diaz politely suppressed a sigh. "I see from your card that you're an advocate or whatever from Edinburgh. That's the Scottish equivalent to a barrister, right? I'm not sure how they do things in Scotland, but here in the States, vacationing lawyers don't have license to trespass on crime scenes."

"I'm also something of a solver of cases." Rex cleared his throat. "At least, I'm getting that reputation," he added modestly.

Diaz didn't look like he was buying any of it. He probably thought the bulky Scotsman with the red hair and beard was one of those loonies or self-appointed psychics who appeared in every sensational case. An apparent double homicide involving a couple of senior citizens dressed as clowns certainly qualified as sensational in Rex's own opinion.

"You may have heard of the multiple murders at Swanmere Manor in England some Christmases ago," Rex said, hoping on the off chance that the case had made American headlines.

"Can't say that I have." The detective wore polarizing sunglasses suspended from his neck. He adjusted the black lanyard around his crisp white collar and asked, "Where exactly were you last night, Mr. Graves, if you were not here?"

"On the Atlantic Ocean somewhere between Miami and Key West. Our ship docked off Mallory Square early this morning for a day of sightseeing. My fiancée and I were on our way to the Hemingway Home when we got lost and saw the police cars barricading the street."

Much as Rex wanted to see where Ernest Hemingway had resided, it could wait. This couldn't. He didn't believe fate had brought him to this location at this precise moment so he could help solve the case, but now he was here, he could not imagine being anywhere else.

Just then a pony-tailed videographer with "Crime Scene Unit" in white lettering on the back of his blue shirt entered the kitchen by the interior door, almost sideswiping Rex with the equipment perched on his shoulder.

"About time," Diaz said.

"Traffic was brutal. What we got? A coupla clowns?"

"Just get on with it, Tony."

Rex retreated into the breakfast nook as Tony took his wide angle views before moving in closer to the bodies. "Dead sometime after midnight, I'd say," he muttered crookedly beneath the video camera.

"You're not paid to say," Diaz stated. "That's for the medical examiner to determine. Just record the scenery."

"Just sayin'. They don't look like they're in full rigor yet. And get a load of this." Tony let out a low whistle as he crouched beside the corpses. "Identical bowlines around the necks and wrists."

"Yup," Diaz agreed. "Nautical knots. But that don't advance us much. Most everybody on this island knows something about knots. My ten year-old can rig up one of those."

Not me, thought Rex, standing as inconspicuously as his hulking size allowed. As he took in the conversation, he made a mental inventory of the kitchen, from the huge aluminum sink to the iron skillets hanging in order of size beneath the hood of the range. Equipment sufficient to service a dozen or more guests, he calculated—in keeping with the size of the B & B. In the old scullery by the door squatted a massive washer and dryer. A handy place to hide perhaps?

"No apparent wounds or signs of hanky-panky," Tony continued. "It all seems real clean and tidy. In fact, looks staged, if you ask me."

"I didn't ask you," Captain Diaz retorted, but this time with a smile.

Tony peered behind the clowns' backs. "Nice job bagging the hands."

"Thanks."

Rex could not see the victims' hands from his vantage point. Diaz would have put clean paper bags fastened with tape over them to preserve possible trace evidence and prevent contamination. Rex hoped one of the clowns had put up a struggle and left the killer's DNA under the finger nails. He felt a tingle of excitement. There was nothing as thrilling as being on the trail of a killer, except perhaps prosecuting that person, which was his official job. He had investigated a murder in Florida once before, at his son's college, where the victim's parents had retained his services, entreating him to seek justice for their one and only son.

"Who's the dude?" Tony asked, looking up at Rex from his video camera.

"He's just leaving," Diaz said pointedly.

Rex took the hint and left.

He had no intention, however, of vacating the premises. While he entertained certain misgivings about staying in accommodation where two alleged murders had taken place, he had, after all, done so before—and had even been able to prevent further casualties. Not that further casualties were to be anticipated in this case, he ruminated, although one could never be sure.

## ~THREE~

Weighing the likelihood of further murders, Rex had come across a slope-shouldered man of middle years hovering outside the yellow-taped door leading into the kitchen. His first impression was of someone soft and doughy, rather like prepackaged white bread.

"Can I help you?" the man asked in a reedy voice. "I'm Walt, the manager. Well, actually the owner now." He said this as though confronting a hard-to-acknowledge fact.

Rex assessed the individual more closely: podgy midsection, thinning hair of graying brown, Buddy Holly glasses obscuring the upper side of his face. His plaid sport shirt exuded a smell of warm toast, and he wore a pair of old loafers.

"Sorry to hear aboot your parents," Rex commiserated as they moved along the dim passage and through the baize door leading into the main part of the guest house. The hall and narrow foyer were painted the same pale purple as the façade. The transom window above the front door irradiated color: a trio of leaping blue dolphins, curving waves in seafoam, a pearl white sky, and a yellow sun.

"Is that a Scots accent?" the innkeeper asked, pleased when Rex confirmed his guess with a nod.

"Are you still open for business?"

"You need a room?" the man asked in surprise. "I'd be more than happy to accommodate you."

Rex thought Walt was taking the deaths of his parents rather well. He had not so much as acknowledged the fact of their demise. "Only if it's not an imposition. The room is for myself and my fiancée."

"No imposition," the man said obsequiously. "None at all. And it helps to keep busy. This is what my parents would have wanted. It's my way of honoring them."

This was said respectfully and without any show of emotion. Rex supposed everyone expressed their grief differently. He wondered how he would feel if his mother died; though, since she was approaching ninety, it was, sadly, more a question of when. "What are your rates?" he asked.

Walt shuffled to the reception desk, which stood in a corner of the foyer by the front door. It resembled a pulpit and supported a large guest book, a roll of paper towels, and a polished chrome bell in the shape of a maple leaf, with a push-knob at the top. Rex supposed the deceased owners had brought this item with them from Vermont.

"The Tennessee Williams Suite just became available," the innkeeper said. "The two sisters—spinster librarians—were staying here on a literary tour, but are leaving. The Robert Frost Suite is vacant, but that faces the street. The Tennessee is one of our nicest. I could get it made up right away and give you a twenty percent discount owing to the inconvenience of law enforcement being here. But they'll be confined to that part of the house." Walt pointed to the baize door through which he and Rex had entered the hall. "They've already interviewed our few guests. Not that it was any of them!" he hastened to add.

He tore off a square of paper towel along the perforation and blotted his brow.

"I would have thought you'd be fully booked for Fantasy Fest," Rex remarked, looking about the narrow space encumbered by a steep flight of stairs.

"Uh, not quite full." Walt plucked at invisible lint on his plaid sport shirt. "The spinsters. Two college students. And the Shumakers from Ohio. A real nice middle-aged couple." He gazed expectantly at Rex as though the Scotsman and his fiancée might find instantaneous friendship in the Shumakers. "Oh, I almost forgot," he added, his face brightening. "We have a couple of writers from Kansas. A man-and-wife writing team. And a businessman by the name of Mr. Bill Reid, but he keeps himself very much to himself."

The innkeeper turned the guest register to face Rex. "If you could just fill in the blanks..."

"Rex Graves is the name, but I had better clear it with my fiancée first. It's ultimately her decision. We're supposed to be on a cruise to Mexico, though I'd just as soon stop in Key West for a few days, if I can get out of it."

"Which cruise line?"

"Carnival. The *Fantasia*."

"Leave it to me. I'll call them and see what I can do."

"Thanks so much," Rex said, assuming the innkeeper had more experience with travel arrangements than he had. "I'll be back." He paused with his hand on the front door knob. "I hope you don't mind my asking, but Helen will want to know what happened, and whether it's safe to stay here."

The two clowns had looked more like realistic wax replicas at Madame Tussaud's in London than actual dead bodies. And Captain Diaz appeared to have everything under control. All the same, he should find out as much as he could before committing himself to a reservation.

"Believe me, the murderer isn't one of the

18

guests," Walt assured him for the second time. "And the only other person staying at the Dolphin Inn is my sister Diane—and her two kids," he added as a quick aside while fumbling with the guest register. "I'm sure the killer has long since skipped town."

Rex sincerely hoped not. America was a big place, and he had no intention of going after the killer all the way to Kansas, or wherever. He was not sure he could even find Kansas on the map in a hurry.

"But what was the motive?" he asked Walt speculatively. And, he pondered, could one person have subdued the owners of the Dolphin Inn, even if they were an older couple?

"You get your fair share of psychos in Key West," Walt said. "Might've been a random mugging. Or drug-related. Who knows with these addicts? They don't even know themselves what they're doing most of the time."

Rex thought this doubtful as the murders had appeared very methodical. "Was anything stolen?" he asked.

"No, actually, and that is a bit odd, isn't it? Look, don't worry about your stuff. There's a safe in every room."

Rex hoped other security precautions were in place too.

"Oh, that's them now!" Walt blurted, his face blanching to a ghostly pallor as he directed his gaze toward the staircase.

Two elderly ladies picked their way down the stairs, the plumper of the pair carrying the bags while the other negotiated the steps, a bony hand on the banister, a walking stick in the other. Since Walt was doing a good impersonation of a petrified rabbit and made no effort to move, Rex rushed to offer assistance, which the ladies blindly ignored.

"My sister and I are leaving now and we demand a refund," said the one with the cane, dressed much like the other in sensible flat shoes, dark velour pants, and a sateen lavender blouse. Though her words made it apparent she was addressing Walt, her eyes through the lenses of her pince-nez were cross-eyed, and it was impossible to tell for sure where she was looking. Pigeon-toed, she bore down on the reception desk with the aid of her walnut cane. Rex stood aside to give the women more room in the cramped hallway.

"I'm afraid I can't offer you a refund," Walt stammered, cowering in his corner.

"Of course you can. Can't he, Emily?"

"I should think so!" said the elderly woman in the pale blue blouse. "A double homicide, the police questioning us endlessly... We could have been murdered in our beds!"

"Quite so, Emily. But what can you expect in this town? Fantasy Fest! Positively heathen. And now our vacation is ruined. Perfectly ruined!"

"Circumstances beyond the guest house's control," Walt ventured, his body trembling like Jell-O. "But perhaps—"

"We are volunteer librarians, with limited funds. We must find another place to stay at short notice. The inconvenience. Isn't that so, Emily?"

If only the Brimstone sisters had researched their destination more carefully, Rex reflected. "Forgive me," he intervened. "But if you cannot be prevailed upon to stay, might I suggest you take your business elsewhere, as you propose, with minimum fuss. This man has just lost his parents and finds himself more inconvenienced than yourselves, surely."

Not-Emily stared in his general direction. "And who are you?"

"A guest here."

"Well, more fool you, I say. Isn't that right, Emily? However, we will pay our bill in full to avoid further unpleasantness."

With a shaking hand, Walt swiped the card through his portable machine and gave the cross-eyed lady the receipt to sign, which she managed to do without missing. He stapled the customer copy to the invoice. "May I call you a cab?"

"No need. And we won't be back," she shrilled.

Rex obligingly opened the front door, and her sister followed with the bags.

They would not have made congenial

companions. He hoped the other guests were more so. Walt mopped his moist brow with the paper towel and thanked Rex for coming to his rescue. Rex felt he'd had little choice. The poor man had been on the verge of a heart attack.

"Och, a harmless pair of old biddies," he said. "Bark worse than their bite. I'll see you in a while."

He stepped out the door, turning to close it. Walt was gazing after him quite pitifully, as though he might never see his potential guest and savior again.

# ~FOUR~

Walt was no longer at reception when Rex returned after seeing Helen off on her shopping spree. It had been touch and go convincing her to stay at the Dolphin Inn, when the owners had been served up for breakfast in their own kitchen, their grotesquely made-up faces preserved in plastic wrap. But fortunately, she had not seen them. He would try and make up for the cruise.

Hearing voices from the room to his right, he found an older couple seated at table having breakfast. The dining room accommodated eight round tables covered with floral tablecloths, fresh posies in vases placed in the center. White crown molding decorated the pale lilac walls, putting Rex in mind of icing on a cake.

The couple looked up from a street map spread out between them as he entered. They wore white shirts with ruffles down the front, red neckerchiefs, and black boleros. Rex assumed they were dressed up as pirates, and this was confirmed when he saw a gold-braided tricorn hat perched on the finial of a spare chair, a fake black beard and a sword lying across the seat. Apparently, Fantasy Fest wasn't over quite yet.

"Is Walt aboot?" he asked in his Scots burr.

"He went to the pastry shop on Duval," said the pixie-haired woman, who was in her late fifties, judging more from the silver streaks in her hair than her smooth skin and slim figure. "The kitchen is sealed off while the crime scene technicians finish up, so no hot breakfast today. We're having ours late because of all the hoopla."

"There's cereal over on that table and hot coffee in the urn." This from her partner, a man of similar age with a sallow complexion and a gray goatee, which failed to disguise his weak chin.

Rex thanked him and helped himself to a mug of coffee. The serving table ran alongside the interior wall of the dining room next to an elegant marble fireplace in pinkish white, heavily carved with a grape motif and topped with a sculpted mantelpiece. He added cream from a jug and two packets of raw sugar from the assortment of sweeteners in a basket.

"Are you staying here?" the woman inquired, gazing at him through her sleek designer spectacles. "I don't recall seeing you before."

"Hoping to stay. I spoke to Walt a short while

24

ago regarding a reservation."

"Are you a reporter?" asked the man, his deep and resonant voice at odds with his undistinguished features. "Can't imagine anyone wanting to stay here otherwise."

"No-oh." Rex drew out the word cautiously. "I'm not a reporter. But there are not many vacancies in Key West at the moment."

"That's the truth," the woman said. "But people will start leaving now the parade is over. And, speaking for ourselves, we find the murder aspect quite exciting! I mean, it's not likely to happen again with all the cops about, and it must have been someone who is miles away by now."

Rex selected a chair at a neighboring table, eager to pursue the topic of murder in the hope of new information. "I take it the owners are Walt's parents?"

"Yes, it's horrible. Of course, I don't want to speak ill of the dead, especially under their own roof, but Taffy Dyer was a piece of work— though I do feel bad for her long-suffering husband."

The woman's companion took her hand and gave it a brief consoling squeeze. They wore identical wedding bands. Rex decided it was time to introduce himself. She beamed at him and said they were Peggy and Dennis Barber from Wichita, Kansas. A few minutes ensued while she finished her muesli and Dennis his cornflakes.

"I hope Walt won't be long. We have a book signing at ten," she said.

"Not much longer," her husband assured her. "He took his moped."

"Are you the writers?" Rex asked. "Walt mentioned something to that effect."

"We are," Peggy all but gushed. "I don't suppose you've heard of us. We write the High Seas Pirate series. It follows the adventures of a seventeenth century buccaneer."

Hence the outfits, Rex surmised.

"The costumes are a bit gimmicky, but it helps sell books," Peggy echoed his thoughts. "The latest novel, which we're here to promote, is *The British Brigand*. We're doing stores in Key West. Borders Express closed, more's the pity. Will you come to our Island Books signing today? It's on Fleming Street."

"I'd love to," Rex prevaricated, "However, I'm going to be rather occupied." He saw the disappointment in Peggy's face. "But if you have a spare copy of your novel, I'd love to buy one and have you sign it."

"Of course!" She reached into a large case on the floor and pulled out a trade paperback with a busy cover. "Who should we dedicate it to?"

"To Helen—my fiancée."

They autographed it, and Dennis reached over the intervening table and presented it to him.

"Oh, aye, verra nice," Rex said, reviewing the

swarthy pirate standing astride the quarterdeck of a captured Spanish galleon. He turned the book over, aghast when he saw the price. He handed over a twenty dollar bill, waving away the offer of small change due on the purchase.

"Are you staying in Key West for long?" Peggy inquired, quick green eyes flashing with interest.

"Not sure yet. We were on our way to Mexico via Miami, where we saw my son briefly. He's pursuing his studies in Jacksonville. But we may stop here for a week."

"Before Key West, we were signing in St. Augustine, another popular venue for pirate fans. That's just an hour from Jax. There's a tradition of pirates and smugglers in Key West, as you'd expect from its proximity to Cuba and Mexico's Yucatan Peninsula."

"Rum from Cuba during Prohibition and drugs from South America," Dennis contributed. "Cannabis and cocaine, mostly."

"Key West had an active drug-trafficking community in the seventies and eighties," Peggy elaborated. "The authorities have really clamped down, but with thousands of boats to and from the island, and millions of tourists pouring in and out each year, law enforcement can't realistically search every vessel and vehicle. And the delays wouldn't be good for tourism. Oh, I think that's Walt now." She craned her neck toward the white gauze draping the bay window.

A whine outside similar to a yard trimmer gave way to a faint rumble and stutter above the chatter of pedestrians waiting for the latest news on the murders.

Peggy's husband checked his watch. "About time."

A few minutes later Walt appeared with a clear plastic-covered tray of pastries, which he placed on the long table. He smiled in relief when he saw Rex.

"Victorian?" The Scotsman leaned back in his chair and pointed to the arched opening of the fireplace mantel culminating in a carved pineapple.

"Circa eighteen hundred and sixty-five. The owl andirons are slightly later."

The cast-iron log supports featured big round eyes glowing amber in the gloom of the swept hearth. From a pewter holder hung a set of fireplace tools—long-handled brush, shovel, poker, and prongs. Rex found it hard to imagine a blazing fire in Florida, but no doubt there were occasions for it.

"The Tennessee Williams Suite is ready, and I called the cruise line," the innkeeper informed him while the Barbers gravitated toward the pastries, Peggy's boyish frame clad in black knickerbockers, her husband in flared black trousers reaching mid-calf. Both were shod in buckled shoes.

"You simply need to see the purser on your ship and fill out some forms. I mean, it's not like they can hold you against your will. Anyway, I told them it was a family emergency." Walt coughed in apology. "Hope that's okay."

"There is a family emergency," Rex replied. "I'm just sorry it happens to be yours."

"You are bearing up amazingly well, Walt," Peggy interjected as she passed on her way back to her table, nibbling on a flaky croissant.

"The show must go on," Walt crowed. "My parents wouldn't want it any other way."

"Of course not," Peggy consoled him. "And you'll do just fine running this place. We have every confidence in you."

Dennis gave Walt a reassuring prod on the shoulder as he, too, returned to their table where they gathered up their belongings. "Duty calls!" he announced, taking his fruit tartlet with him.

"Good luck," Walt called after them. "Our resident writers," he told Rex. "Ah, I see you have one of their books." He looked even more pleased—until Captain Diaz appeared in the doorway.

"Mr. Dyer, you got a minute?" the detective summoned, acknowledging Rex with a brief nod.

Walt gazed back at Rex. "Are you staying?" he asked.

"Aye, don't worry. I'll have one of those delicious-looking pastries and finish my coffee while I wait."

His host gestured toward a wooden rack stacked with fresh newspapers. "Help yourself."

The papers did not yet contain stories of the double homicide at the Dolphin Inn. Headlines abounded about the Fantasy Fest parade. Rex pulled out a copy of *The Citizen*, envisioning the cover page in the next edition: "Local Innkeepers Murdered at B & B!" or "Clowns Involved in Bizarre Death!" No doubt the editors would come up with something more imaginative, but that would be the gist. He wondered what details had been released to the press.

Rex lifted the lid off the pastry tray and selected a chocolate-filled croissant, and returned to his table to enjoy his breakfast while he waited for Helen. His Key West vacation had truly begun and was shaping up to be most interesting. Most interesting indeed.

# ~FIVE~

Rex rose from the table with his empty coffee cup and twitched aside the gauze drapes to take a look at developments outside the bay window. The crowd had expanded to include TV news vans with unfamiliar call letters, one in the process of uploading its live-cam apparatus toward the blurry blue sky. Reporters and cameramen stood about chatting, waiting for further action and comment from anyone willing to offer any. He spotted a patch of yellow approaching down the leafy street. Helen. As she drew nearer, he saw she was holding an assortment of carrier bags. He went out the front door to help her.

The cop at the white picket gate flexed his impressive muscles as Rex relieved her of her bags and guided her up the short flight of steps into the B & B, away from the media calling after her for information.

"Phew! Talk about running the gauntlet," she said. "I insisted I didn't know anything beyond what they already knew."

She looked around the pale purple walls of the lobby. "Interesting choice of colour," she remarked with a surprised grimace that said it all. "Thank you for the use of your credit card." She pulled out a two-foot papier-mâché flamingo.

"What's that for?"

"I don't know. I just couldn't resist. I can put it in my office." She plunged into another bag and produced a straw hat with a blue bow matching her eyes.

"Well, that's functional, at least."

She put it on and posed.

"And verra fetching," he complimented in broad Scots.

"I got one for you too." She dug out a straw boater. "You always forget to put on sun cream. This will help."

His delicate fair skin, the curse of a redhead, was prone to turning the shade of a boiled lobster after only one hour in the sun.

"I have a souvenir for you too," he said. "It's a pirate novel."

Helen regarded the book with curiosity. "Just look at the rippling pecs on *him*," she exclaimed, and laughed. "Where on earth did you find it?"

"From the husband-and-wife team of authors staying at the Dolphin Inn. See here," he said opening it to the inside title page. "It has a special dedication."

" 'To Helen, with all best wishes for a happy stay in Key West,' " she read. "What are D. and P. Barber like?"

"Dennis and Peggy. She's nice, Dennis is a bit taciturn. They're from the Midwest."

"How exciting. I've never met a real novelist before." She removed her straw hat. "Where's the innkeeper?"

"He's being questioned by the detective, but he said he contacted the cruise line and it was a straightforward enough procedure to get off the ship for good. I suggest we provisionally reserve our suite and then go and see about getting our luggage."

"Have you seen our room?"

Rex admitted he had not, but that it was ready.

"As long as you're sure," Helen said redirecting her gaze at the lilac paint on the walls.

"Come and take a look at the Victorian fireplace." Rex knew she would like the carved grapes and ribbons on the mantel. He led her into the dining room.

"Well, this is nice," she approved, taking in the floral tablecloths and black-and-white prints on the walls depicting Key West before the advent of color photography.

While she was admiring the fireplace, he heard a distant door creak open and two male voices growing in volume. The first, pleasantly modulated, he recognized as belonging to Captain Diaz. The second was saying, "Walt Dyer is insisting he stayed home. Doesn't like the noise and crowds at these events. But a guy in a neighboring apartment noticed Walt's moped missing from its usual spot when he returned home at about one this morning. Diane Dyer says she was asleep upstairs with her kids." The voices disappeared through the front door, which closed with a soft thud. Footsteps retreated down the brick path.

"It's a pinkish shade I've heard referred to as 'blush,' " Helen remarked looking over her shoulder at the marble mantel as she and Rex returned to the foyer. "And aren't those owls a hoot?" she asked, referring to the andirons.

He laughed at her joke. Just then, Walt emerged through the baize door camouflaged in lilac that led to the kitchen annex. He appeared delighted to see them.

"Ah, there you are," he said.

"How did it go?" Rex asked.

"Just a formality." Walt fidgeted with a loose thread on his plaid shirt. "Captain Diaz wanted to know if my parents always participated in the parade, and what time they left. That sort of stuff."

He held out a hairless, pudgy hand to Helen. Rex guessed it would feel clammy to the touch, and, sure enough, Helen surreptitiously wiped her palm against her dress as soon as Walt's back was turned.

"Let me show you around," he said, and suggested his guests leave the shopping bags behind the reception desk.

He led them down the hall past the padded door to the back of the establishment and presented the guest lounge. A sofa and matching armchairs in purple leather dominated a room decorated with wild animal paintings of zebras and lions on pale fuchsia walls. Rex winced. There was no accounting for taste, as his mother liked to say. Helen stared in barely disguised horror.

"You can make tea and coffee here whenever you like." The innkeeper indicated an alcove fitted with a mini fridge, microwave, and counter top on which rested a coffee machine and a set of mugs studded with blue enamel dolphins. "You get to keep one of these mugs when you leave, as a memento of your stay at the Dolphin Inn."

"How nice," Helen said in what appeared to Rex to be genuine appreciation.

Walt explained that a friend of his hand-crafted them in his studio. He proceeded to open a sliding glass door. "Out here is our pool, hot tub, and tiki bar. The gate from the alley was bolted last night. The cops scoured this area and found nothing, so feel free to use it."

The pool was private and sheltered from the

breeze by a tall stockade fence, though a breeze would be welcome today, Rex thought. It felt uncomfortably warm and close. Walt untucked the front of his plaid shirt and flapped it to let in some air.

The fence, draped with pink bougainvillea and oleander, screened the B & B from the property behind, whose tin roof peeked out above red-canopied Royal Poinciana in late bloom. The trees must be under irrigation to be flowering so late, Rex reflected, and were not as showy as some he had seen in Florida. Still, they added a nice splash of color.

Walt stepped onto the patio deck surrounding the kidney-shaped pool, where two children squabbled over a raft. The boy, a stick insect of about eight years old, wore plastic green goggles that gave him the look of a demented frog. He tried frantically to dislodge a chubby girl in a red polka dot swimsuit from the raft. "Those are my sister's kids," Walt explained. "Justin and Kylie."

"Mom!" the girl wailed at a scrawny blonde stretched out on a padded lounge chair smoking a cigarette. "Tell Justin to quit!"

"Justin, what did Nana say about trying to drown your sister?" The woman in dark sunglasses spoke without looking up from her magazine.

"Nana's dead. I'm glad she's dead. She was mean!"

"Shut your mouth," the girl squealed, dunking his head under the water.

Rex watched to make sure he resurfaced, which he did a moment later, gasping and spluttering, wet hair flattened over his skull. To the right of the pool lay a below-ground hot tub covered with blue canvas. Between it and the building stood a frond-thatched tiki bar, lending a tropical aspect to the area of poured concrete. Pottery urns containing hibiscus and dwarf citrus trees lined the fence on that side, while the fence opposite blocked out the alley.

Walt padded back into the guest lounge, pausing to allow his guests to catch up. "Diane just got through a nasty divorce," he confided.

Not to mention her parents' death, Rex thought, although Diane seemed no more upset than her brother.

"Terrible what you must be going through, losing your parents so suddenly," Helen commiserated.

Walt rubbed at a non-existent stain on the back of the plush purple sofa. The guest house was spic and span, almost antiseptically so. "Sudden, yes," their host mused aloud. "I'll have to make arrangements with Pritchard Funeral Home. Hmm." He stood gazing at the ground, vague and confused. Rex had noticed that Walt rarely made eye contact.

Helen raised her eyebrow at Rex. He knew

exactly what she was thinking: Why had they foregone cocktails on the Lido Deck to stay in a purple B & B that had housed two dead bodies and was plagued by two shrieking brats intent on drowning each other?

"My parents had so much to live for," Walt warbled on, as if to himself. "They were getting ready to retire. They were really looking forward to it."

"How sad. Were they in good health?" Helen asked.

"Perfect health for their age, except for the fact that Taffy's liver wasn't in the best shape."

Rex found it curious that Walt should refer to his mother as Taffy. Or perhaps it was just a convenient form of address, since he and his parents had run the B & B together. Perhaps it sounded more professional and had become force of habit.

"Merle gave up his job as an accountant when they opened their first guest house in Vermont. It gave Taffy something to do, and he was able to keep more of an eye on her. She, um, liked to drink." A mottled blush crept up his neck.

"What were your parents going to do about the guest house when they retired?" Rex asked.

"Sell it."

"Will you keep the Dolphin Inn going now?" Helen inquired.

"Of course. Though I'll need more help. We

had a reliable person working here until Taffy fired him a week ago."

"Why was he fired if he was reliable?" Rex asked. "Was it so your sister could replace him?"

"Oh, no. Diane is feeling very fragile since her divorce. She helps when she can, but the kids take up a lot of energy when they're not at school. Taffy plain didn't like Raphael. No reason given. No severance pay, nothing. She even refused to give him a reference."

"That seems a bit harsh." Rex was beginning to see why the Dyers had been so unpopular.

"And the guests liked Raf," Walt said in a reminiscing tone. "I think that's what got to her. He could mix drinks like nobody's business and we'd set up music out by the tiki bar. She threatened to report him to Immigration Services if he made trouble."

Rex wondered if the detective was aware of Raphael's unjust termination. A disgruntled employee had a motive for murder. "Maybe now you can hire him back," he suggested.

"Don't know where he went. Raf's from El Salvador. He was an undocumented worker we paid under the table." Walt glanced anxiously at Rex then, as if regretting his loose tongue.

"Fear not," Rex assured him. "I won't report it. For one thing, it's none of my business." Murder might be, but not how people chose to run their bed-and-breakfasts, however illegal.

The innkeeper proffered a weak smile in gratitude and led them up the stairs, turning left off the landing into a short, carpeted corridor. A wooden plaque on the door designated it as the Tennessee Williams Suite in a black scroll font. "All our rooms are named for illustrious writers associated with Key West," he explained, casting open the door. "There's a decanter of sherry on the dresser and cookies every night when we turn down the beds."

The decor inside the hardwood floor suite was white and shades of blue, Rex was relieved to see, and a marked improvement on their cabin. Dominating the room, a queen-size four poster bed displayed a patchwork quilt and a decorative, bead-trimmed mosquito net suspended from a hoop in the white-paneled ceiling. Beyond a set of billowy white drapes, a narrow balcony accommodated a pair of blue-cushioned wicker rocking chairs overlooking the pool and bougainvillea cascading over the fence on the far property line. A pair of Ringed Turtle-Doves disputed ownership of a Poinciana branch, creating quite a commotion. Rex, a keen bird-watcher, thought it would enjoyable to watch them from time to time from the balcony.

In the en-suite bathroom, framed samplers exhorted guests to unwind, drink in abundance, and generally forget their worldly cares. Orange hibiscus petals lay scattered in the tub—a nice touch, he further observed.

He hazarded a glance at Helen, who nodded with enthusiasm. "We'll take it," he said, consulting her with another look to make sure. Walt was an oddball to be sure, but an oddball who couldn't say boo to a goose, let alone two little old ladies. "As long as the cruise line doesn't make difficulties," he added. "This will do us fine."

He congratulated himself that everything was going according to plan so far. Hopefully it would be goodbye "Fun Ship" and hello, Key West and the Dolphin Inn!

# ~SIX~

The procedure for permanent disembarkation took longer than expected, but the Carnival staff was courteous, as had been Rex's experience for the short extent of the cruise. When he and Helen finally returned to the B & B in a cab with their luggage and had unpacked, they were in no mood for any strenuous sightseeing. And now there was no rush. They decided to walk to Sloppy Joe's Bar and grab a late lunch.

A few gawkers remained outside the Dolphin Inn, Key West's latest attraction. Tourists snapped pictures while locals passed by with quizzical expressions. There was nothing much left to see. The emergency vehicles had departed with the bodies and crews, and no one had been led away in handcuffs, as far as Rex knew. As he and Helen exited the B & B and walked down the path in their new straw hats, a heavyset man in a long-billed cap had the audacity to take their picture.

"Fame at last," Helen said.

"I feel like a tourist in this hat."

"You are a tourist," she reminded him.

On Duval the sidewalks streamed with boisterous tourists. He and Helen headed north past the Eaton and Caroline Street intersections to Greene Street, where Sloppy Joe's took up the entire corner. Helen, who liked to read up on her holiday destinations, explained that the name of the bar had been suggested by Ernest Hemingway to friend and owner Joe Russell, a charter boat captain, speakeasy operator, and rum-runner during Prohibition. Inside the rectangular building, the dim interior was filled with occupied wooden tables, bustle and noise.

Photographs, paintings, and news clippings commemorated the city's most famous resident and his beloved sport-fishing boat, *Pilar*. The bar even sold T-shirts featuring the writer's bearded face. From what Rex had seen of Key West, almost everywhere sold T-shirts, and most everything had received the distinction of "World Famous." Key West was unashamedly touristy since the cigar and sponge industries had moved to Tampa before the Great Depression, causing the once prosperous city to go bankrupt, as Helen had informed him on their walk from the Dolphin Inn.

Rex could not think of a better place to relax

than on this palm-festooned island, forming a pendant in a turquoise sea at the end of a string of keys. The main objective in Key West was to have a good time, aided by a drink or two. And when in Rome…

They selected the last vacant table at the far side of the reggae duo on stage. Paddle fans on a cavernous ceiling strung with international flags rotated warm beery air and the aroma of deep fry. A fake Blue Marlin hovered incongruously above a case exhibiting a pair of old-fashioned skis. Helen ordered a Papa Dobles daiquiri, a favorite drink of Hemingway's from Cuba, she further informed Rex, who stuck with Guinness.

"Let the holiday truly begin!" she toasted, raising her plastic cup.

Rex sat forward on his stool, forearms on the table. "I'll call Campbell and see if he can fly down here. He's never been to Key West. If you recall, we stayed further up the Keys a few years ago, but never made it all the way down."

"That's when you solved the murder at his college, and the victim's parents lent you their beach cottage in Islamorada."

"And their boat. It was a memorable time. Campbell and I had a lot of catching up to do." Rex polished off his stout and let out a satisfied sigh. "I sometimes think it would be nice to retire to Florida."

"Will you tell him about the murders?" Helen

asked.

"I'll have to. He'll want to know why we're not in Mexico. But he probably won't be able to get down until the weekend."

"You feel confident you'll have solved the case by then?" Helen twiddled her straw in the ice-diluted concoction of rum and ruby red grapefruit and cherry juice left at the bottom of her glass. She fished out her wedge of lime and proceeded to nibble on it.

"That's my goal." Rex ordered fresh drinks and basket food. He adored American fries, and decided not to stint on calories while on vacation. It wouldn't be nearly as much as they served on the cruise, he rationalized, where the temptation of food leaped out at you everywhere.

"Any ideas yet?" Helen asked, returning to the topic of the murders once the young server had left with their orders. "It could have been just about anyone on the island."

"Anyone with a grudge."

"Not a random act then?"

Rex shook his head. "No, it was too methodical by half. Premeditated, even."

"Wouldn't it have made more sense from the killer's perspective to make it look like a bungled mugging?"

"Aye, it would."

Rex gave this scenario due consideration. He tried to put himself in the mind of the killer. Was a bold statement being made? A murder in the victims' home and place of work would create more buzz than a random attack in the street. He wondered whether Captain Diaz had drawn the same conclusions.

Ripples of applause for the live band punctuated the conversations and bursts of laughter resounding around the saloon. In eager anticipation, Rex watched his Guinness approach on a tray, condensation beading the cold glass. The muggy weather made him thirsty.

"Well, I'm glad you found something suitably morbid to occupy your time," Helen said as her cocktail was deposited before her and the empty cup swept away. "Since you don't play golf, I can just tell everybody I'm a murder widow," she joked, her cheeks dimpling impishly.

"You don't mind too much?" he pleaded as qualms of conscience resurfaced. After all, Helen had planned the cruise for him as a semi-surprise.

"Not too much," she said. "I'll be perfectly happy to sunbathe by the pool and read while you're investigating. Or find a beach on the island."

Key West disposed of a handful of small beaches where imported sand covered the sharp native coral. The one at Fort Zachary Taylor State Park was closest to where they were staying, and bikes could be rented from various locations, Walt had informed them. Helen did not feel as though she'd had a proper vacation until she experienced the sensation of sand sifting between her toes. Beach holidays, however, were not particularly Rex's thing.

He took her hand and kissed it. "I'm at your complete disposal for the next few hours," he promised.

And a fun few hours it proved to be as they enjoyed the rowdy ambiance of Sloppy Joe's before strolling back to the Dolphin Inn along tranquil tree-shaded streets, admiring the Conch architecture characterized by colorful Bermuda shutters and wide wood porches. Larger dwellings, many of them ornate clapboard mansions built by nineteenth century sea captains, merchants and wreckers, several of which had been converted into guest houses, set adrift sweet botanical scents as they passed the front yards.

The lilac façade of the Dolphin Inn looped in fluorescent yellow tape appeared as a mirage in the shimmering heat of midafternoon. A single news van remained parked on the street. An officer guarded the entranceway to the alley leading to the B & B's kitchen. These signs, in stark contrast with the jovial atmosphere of Duval Street, reminded Rex that death tainted the walls of the guest house, and that some spur-of-the-moment folly had prompted him to tread where he had little business doing so. Still, he thought; too late to change course now. He would solve the case come hell or high water, or the specter of the aborted cruise would surely come back to haunt him.

Helen might never forgive him.

## ~SEVEN~

After sleeping off the restorative lunch at Sloppy Joe's, Rex crept out of bed while Helen napped on, all thoughts of Mexico gone from her head, or so he hoped. She really was a good sport, and he resolved to take her on the honeymoon of her dreams to make up for the abandoned cruise.

He decided to call his son right away and tell him about their change of plan, wondering as he descended the stairs what Campbell's reaction would be to news of his father's self-appointed involvement in the clown murders.

"Mind if I call Jacksonville on your house phone?" he asked Walt at the foot of the stairs. "I didn't bring my mobile—my cell phone—with me to the States, and my fiancée is taking a nap."

"Sure thing. Use this one." The innkeeper produced an old black dial phone from behind the pulpit desk and placed it next to the guest book.

"I'll be in the kitchen if you need me. The lab crew left print dust all over that part of the house," he said with tears in his voice. "What a mess!"

He wandered off before Rex could say something comforting. He dialed and reached his son on the second ring. Campbell sounded surprised to hear from his dad, no doubt assuming he was somewhere in the Gulf gazing upon expanses of azure water and real dolphins, unlike the glass ones in the transom.

"We decided to stay in Key West for the rest of the week," Rex explained.

"Yeah? Why?"

"We were seduced by its distinctive character and literary heritage, the whisper of the trade winds blowing through the palms, the—"

"Stop! Seriously, Dad, what are you *smoking?*" During his long stay in the States, Campbell had picked up several American expressions and much of the inflection, but had for the most part retained his fluted Scottish accent, which made for a bizarre combination.

"There was a small matter of a double murder..."

"No way!" A breathless pause on the phone betrayed Campbell's disbelief. "Da-a-d," he warned. "Is Helen okay with this?"

Rex reassured him on this score and asked if Campbell would like to fly down to Key West from Jacksonville next weekend—Dad's treat.

"Whoa... Thing is, Mel might be in town. Could she come?"

"I don't see why not."

"I have lab Friday morning. We could take off soon afterwards. Really, Dad? That would be so cool. By the way, what sort of murders, exactly?"

"A pair of suffocated clowns." That, at any rate, appeared to be the cause of death, and Rex was anxious to find out more.

"Clowns? Like at a circus? You're kidding!"

"They were dressed up for Fantasy Fest."

"You went to Fantasy Fest?" Clearly, Campbell thought his father was losing his marbles. "I heard that's, uh, pretty wild." *For you*, being the implication.

"It was over by the time we arrived," Rex assured him. He didn't want to go into further details about the murders as he was standing in a public foyer, with voices emanating from the guest lounge at the end of the hall. "Take this number down. We're staying at the Dolphin Inn." He gave his son the number and address. "If I'm not here, ask Walt to take a message, and I'll call you back."

"This is such an antiquated arrangement," Campbell said. "Why didn't you bring your cell phone?"

"I didn't think I'd need it in the middle of the Gulf of Mexico, and I couldn't be bothered switching to an international plan for just one week."

"Whatever, Dad." Campbell chuckled. "You are such a Luddite."

"A Luddite who's going to be paying your airfares."

"Point taken. I'll look up the flights. Talk to you soon," Campbell said as though talking through a wide smile. "And thanks!"

Thrilled that he might be seeing his son, Rex replaced the handset and tucked a ten-dollar bill under the guest book to cover the cost of the call. Then, curious to see what sort of comments previous guests had left regarding their sojourn at the Dolphin Inn, he pulled the tome toward him. Most of the entries were short and less than effusive, restricted to "we had a pleasant stay" and "good breakfasts," and similar phrases.

He had frequented enough such establishments to know that the guest book was the Bible of the B & B. Clearly, the Dolphin Inn had not made many converts. One entry clinically stated, "*We were very grateful to Taffy for being able to accommodate our dietary requests.*" Nothing about Merle. However, entries further back in time thanked Raphael for his "extra attentions" and "going the extra mile," and praised his "spectacular margaritas by the pool." One even referred to him as "a gem." These dated from the summer when the elder Dyers must have been in Vermont.

Taffy Dyer had, by Walt's account, turned this 'gem' out onto the street. Rex repositioned the guest book. It was time to talk to people who might have overheard or seen something the previous night that could help lead to a discovery in the case of the murdered owners.

In the guest lounge, he found two couples, one young and one middle-aged, ensconced in the purple furniture. It was happy hour. Walt had said on the tour of the B & B that alcoholic refreshment was provided for the guests, along with a cheese and fruit platter.

Rex helped himself to a glass of California chardonnay standing in a bottle cooler on the counter. In response to the "How ya doin'?" from the man of his age, he introduced himself as Rex Graves, from Edinburgh.

"Scotland, huh?" said the shiny-bald man whose benign expression and heavy jowls reminded Rex of a St. Bernard, and whose Guy Harvey T-shirt stretched over a large beer gut. He held a glass of wine in his hand, which came across as rather incongruous. "Played golf there once," he said. "Where was it now?" He turned to the warmly smiling woman beside him. "St. Andrews," he said before she could reply. "Where Prince William and Kate went to college. That was some royal wedding. My wife was glued to the TV. We're from Dayton, Ohio. Chuck Shumaker. And my better half, Alma."

Alma, wide hips stuffed into shorts, was blessed with a pretty face and a glossy chestnut mane worthy of a shampoo commercial. A well-thumbed paperback by Nora Roberts lay splayed on the sofa beside her. Books with multicolor spines left by previous guests lined the white wood shelves of a cabinet by the coffee machine, as did a selection of DVDs.

"Welcome to the Bates Motel," Mrs. Shumaker joked with a wry smile.

The young couple laughed from across the coffee table, where they sat holding hands on a purple love seat. Rex glanced in their direction and smiled. They were about his son's age and must be the students Walt had referred to earlier when he was listing the guests.

"That Hitchcock movie used to be on the shelf with the others, but now it's disappeared," Alma Shumaker added with an air of mystery. "This is Ryan and his girlfriend, Michelle."

The girl, in a shimmering gold off-the shoulder top, tossed back her long-layered dark hair. Her aquiline nose stood prominent on a pale face that made her dark eyes, heavily rimmed with kohl and mascara, all the more arresting. She reminded him of a sleek animal, rather like one of the feline predators in the oil paintings hanging on the walls. The lad, open-faced and with curly blond hair like Campbell's, grinned in welcome, showing even, ultra-white teeth amid the closely shaved blond bristle. Rex asked which college they attended.

"University of Florida," Ryan replied, followed by a "Go Gators" cheer from Chuck. "How did you know we were students?"

"Walt gave me the lowdown on the guests."

"He's creepy," Michelle said.

"So, what brought you to this house of horrors?" Alma Shumaker inquired. "You must've heard what happened."

"Aye. Most unfortunate, to say the least."

"And it's not a great guest house either."

"Och, it's no that bad," Rex remonstrated in full-blown Scots. "It's comfortable and clean, and the garden is lovely."

"The interior design is, like, hideous," the girl commented, echoing Helen's opinion.

"Well, I cannot disagree with you there."

Michelle smirked, glad, it appeared, to have affirmation.

"When did you get in, Rex?" Chuck asked.

Rex rested his posterior on a plush purple armrest across from the two couples. "Just as the police got here."

"Did you try and get out of your reservation?" Alma Shumaker wanted to know.

Rex decided not to divulge to the guests that the bizarre double murder was the reason for his stay. "Och, it makes for a more interesting holiday," he fudged.

"I'll say," Chuck said with a guffaw, his brown

eyes twinkling above a bulbous nose. "When you get back home, you can tell all your buddies about the cereal killer." He laughed unabashedly at his own humor. "Get it? Bed-and-breakfast serial killer."

Alma, no doubt accustomed to hearing the same old jokes and stock-in-trade responses from her husband, smiled with forbearance. Since the subject was wide open for discussion, Rex plowed right in. "Any idea whodunit?" he asked conspiratorially.

"Walt Dyer," Alma Shumaker whispered loud enough for Rex to hear. "Or else his sister. They're both of them very strange. Not surprisingly, as the elder Dyers were pieces of work, especially Taffy."

Rex remembered that Peggy Barber, the novelist, had said the same thing.

Leaning forward, Alma continued in a low voice. "Taffy...you know..." She tipped her hand toward her mouth to indicate somebody drinking. "She had this fake brightness about her. Never missed happy hour with the guests, but I think she started first thing in the morning with the mimosas."

Chuck nodded sagely. "My cousin's girlfriend has the same problem. He finds empty vodka bottles all over the house. Says he has the problem under control, but if you ask me, it's controlling him too. Alcoholism will do that." He nodded at his own wisdom.

"Yeah, the Dyers were, like, totally weird," Michelle contributed. Her boyfriend, Rex noticed, stared into his wine glass. "Taffy told me she'd found dead cats on the doorstep," she added.

"Sounds like a warning." Rex made himself more comfortable on the armrest and took a sip of the chardonnay. "Did she say how long it had been going on?"

"Since the last week of September, so about a month. She said it started around her birthday."

"Nice present," put in Ryan. "Not."

"Creepy," said Michelle. "Like, who would *do* that?" She had a tendency to pound syllables for emphasis and used the word "like" a lot and unnecessarily, as did so many of her generation, to Rex's chagrin.

"What do you do, Rex?" Chuck asked in an affable manner, leaning back in the sofa and depositing his foot, shod in a white Croc, across a sunburned knee.

"I'm a QC at the High Court of Justiciary in Edinburgh. Queen's Counsel," he explained when he met Ryan's questioning expression. "A prosecutor. So, why is happy hour held in here and not on the back patio? It's a nice, warm evening, after all."

"A bit humid," Alma said. "It does a number on my hair. I think we may get rain, but it never lasts long."

"Beats snow," Chuck Shumaker said.

"Did it rain yesterday night for the parade?" Rex asked, pursuing his quest for background information on the murders.

"No, we lucked out," Chuck said. "Except I was way too hot in my pirate gear."

It came as no surprise to Rex that Chuck Shumaker's lack of originality had prompted him to dress up as a pirate. Alma had been a pirate as well, it transpired, or, as she put it, a pirate's companion in a barmaid's costume.

"Rex here could have worn a kilt!" Chuck said with a guffaw. "Do you have a kilt and one of those furry whaddya-callems?"

"Sporrans. I do, for formal wear."

"That's too funny," Ryan said, grinning.

"And what did you dress up as?" Rex asked the young couple.

"Vampires."

Rex thought Michelle appropriately vampish in her looks, with her dark hair, pale skin, and scarlet lipstick matching the talons on her fingers. Ryan was harder to imagine as a blood-sucking villain.

"Taffy offered us clown costumes," his girlfriend informed Rex. "As *if.*"

"When Taffy was showing Michelle a costume," Alma said, "She turned to me and said, 'I'd loan you one, but none will fit.' " A ruby stain spread across her cheeks.

Chuck groaned. "Talk about tact."

Rex could tell the insult still stung Alma, who tried to disguise her fury with a brittle laugh.

"Perhaps if we all drank our breakfast we could be as thin as her," she remarked, reaching toward the platter of cheese and crackers, and then retracting her hand, as though not wishing to seem greedy and justify Mrs. Dyer's cruel observation.

"She collected clown stuff," Michelle elaborated in a hushed tone. "Clothes, pictures, figurines, anything to do with clowns. You should see her den. She was, like, obsessed with them. Walt has a moth collection. How creepy is that?"

Michelle seemed to find a lot that was creepy. And weird. Rex asked whether Taffy and Merle had lived at the B & B.

"You can tell he's a lawyer!" Chuck said, nudging his wife. "All these questions! They did, but Walt rooms somewhere else." He lowered his voice. "Couldn't stand his parents from what we could see. We'd hear Taffy berating him in the kitchen. Never called her Mom or anything like that. It was always Taffy and Merle. Nothing wrong with that, I guess, but you couldn't exactly feel the love."

"That's what she wanted everyone to call her," Michelle interjected around a mouthful of cracker, brushing crumbs off her short shirt. "Even m—"

Ryan cut her off with a warning look.

"Two-faced is what she was," Alma said,

cautiously looking toward the door to make sure she was not overheard.

"Merle never stood up for his son," her husband remarked. "You got to feel sorry for the poor guy."

"Couldn't stand up for him*self*," Alma corrected in a low voice. "A man of his age in that situation... I mean, thirty-eight! An *old* thirty-eight."

Rex had assumed Walt to be older than that, judging by his looks and mannerisms. He wondered what his childhood had been like.

"And I think he's..." Another hand gesture from Alma, this one limp-wristed.

Rex made further inquiries about Fantasy Fest. Chuck informed him that the highlights of the event were the Masquerade March on Friday and Captain Morgan's float parade the next day. Basically, the October festival was one big street party, where pretty much anything went and the local cops turned a blind eye, unless matters turned violent.

In the tourist brochures, Rex had seen pictures of frenzied crowds with painted bodies of all ages prancing down Simonton Street and the procession of elaborate floats dispensing beads on Duval.

"We were out until maybe three in the morning. It was insane," Ryan said with a reminiscing grin. "Next thing, the cops are hammering on our door waking us up."

"Got in around that time as well," Alma said. "We ran into Michelle and Ryan on Duval around midnight or so, and hung out for a while."

"Hardly recognized them," Ryan said. "Chuck here was Captain Morgan—fake black beard, big boots, coat, the works."

The two couples had the perfect alibi, Rex noted, sipping his wine. Tens of thousands of revelers attended the parade, many in fancy dress. People too numerous to interview, too inebriated to remember, and who had possibly left Key West by now.

"Been staying here long?" he asked the guests.

"Six days. Leaving tomorrow." Chuck anchored himself more firmly into the squashy sofa as though reluctant to leave.

"Us too. Heading back to Gainesville." Ryan yawned. It had obviously been a long night and a tiring day for the young couple. "This is our fourth day."

Rex pulled himself off the armrest and went to refill his glass for Helen, whom he calculated must be stirring by now. Wishing the two couples a pleasant evening, he made his way back down the hall with a clearer picture of the Dyer family dynamics and some valuable insights into the guests.

He recalled there was one other occupant Walt had mentioned, whom he had yet to meet.

# ~EIGHT~

Glass of chardonnay in hand, Rex approached the stairs. A glum Walt sat behind the reception desk on his stool, looking for all the world like an overgrown dunce relegated to a corner of the classroom.

"I wonder if you could recommend somewhere for dinner," Rex inquired. "Perhaps with a view of the water."

"Oh..." Walt came out of his reverie. "Sorry. My single gentleman skipped out without paying his bill, and I was just wondering what to do about it."

"The business man you mentioned?"

"Bill Reid. He was due to leave today. Nice Canadian gentleman. I'm surprised he left without saying goodbye. I can charge his credit card for last night, but I'm not sure when he left. Could have been early this morning when I was busy with the detectives, or else some time yesterday. Taffy would have known as she kept tabs on all the guests. But he never officially checked out, so I can't be sure."

"Are you certain he left?"

"I went into his room a moment ago with clean towels, and all his personal effects are gone. The cops were looking for him, wanting to question him same as everyone else."

"Maybe he got scared off by the murders." Rex thought it fortunate not more guests had booked into the Dolphin Inn. However, the bodies had not been found until seven this morning. The two couples he had just spoken with in the guest lounge were coming to the end of their stay, otherwise they might have checked out early.

"The only people not scared off are the press." Walt ripped a sheet of paper towel off the roll and wiped away at the spotless mahogany surface of the desk. "The first flurry of cancellations has come in. I'm so glad you booked a room. Not sure why you did...considering."

"Well, the, ehm, event occurred in a separate part of the building, after all. And your bed-and-breakfast is nice and central."

"Oh, yes, very convenient. Within walking distance of all the major attractions."

"Quite so." Rex hesitated. He wanted to be upfront about the real reason he was here, or, at least, to not completely dissimulate it. "I should also mention that this is not the first time I find myself in a place where death had occurred." Or the second, third, or fourth.

"Oh, I see." Walt gazed at him questioningly through his black-framed glasses. "Well, that's alright then," he hemmed. "And your fiancée?"

"She's used to it too." Except that in her case, it wasn't a matter of choice. Rex just happened to attract murder like a magnet, as she liked to put it. "And your sister? How is she handling your parents' passing?"

"They weren't close. Diane only came here because she had nowhere else to go after her divorce. She came for some peace and quiet, not that that's happened."

"The publicity will blow over once the culprit or culprits are apprehended," Rex consoled him. "It might even ultimately work to your advantage."

"That's what I've been hoping," Walt said on a pensive note. "A tie-in for Halloween...or a crime scene theme for mystery writers, going forward. Some people go in for that sort of thing."

More to the point, who went in for murder right here in Key West? Rex wondered.

The innkeeper roused himself. "Oh, yes, you were asking about a restaurant. I would recommend Louie's Afterdeck. The food is great, with a terrific view of the ocean, but I believe it's closed for dinner Sundays and Mondays. I'll see if

I can get you a table at The Funky Parrot. It's a lot of fun and very Key West, plus it's closer. Is around seven okay? I'll call your room and let you know."

"That would be grand."

Rex climbed the stairs, pausing when he heard a woman's raspy voice declare, "I'm in the Hemingway Suite. I just know Taffy wanted to stick me and the kids in one of the attic rooms, but how would that have *looked*? Hemingway was married four times and committed suicide, you know. I suppose it could have been worse. My parents could have put me in the McCullers'."

Rex took another step and glimpsed a pair of skinny legs beneath a shapeless gray dress. This must be the Dyers' divorced daughter Diane, whom he had seen at the pool with the two rambunctious kids.

"Oh, I just love *The Heart is a Lonely Hunter*," floated Helen's response from around the corner. "Wonderful characters, especially the deaf mute. I forget his name."

"John Singer. Carson McCullers wrote that when she was twenty-three. She wanted to be a concert pianist, but developed rheumatoid fever at an early age and eventually became paralyzed all down her left side. Every joint in her hand had to be operated on. And she lost her right breast to cancer. At some point she attempted suicide too. Her husband succeeded."

What a depressing conversation, Rex thought, glad they had not been booked into the McCullers' Suite. Or Hemingway's.

"We love our suite," Helen said in an upbeat tone. "Tennessee Williams' house was around here, wasn't it? I'm sure he led a happier life," she trailed off with less assurance in her voice.

"Why would you think that?" Diane inquired. "Have you seen *A Streetcar Named Desire*? All that repressed longing and violence. And the playwright choked to death on a plastic cap from a bottle of eye drops. I think he..."

And Rex had always thought creative writing a hazard-free occupation. Enough! he decided, attacking the final steps before Diane Dyer could spew forth more of her gruesome literary lore. Interrupting the conversation, he said brightly, "Hello. You must be Diane."

"How did you guess?" the woman with the scraggly blond ponytail asked, suspicion narrowing her viper-green eyes.

"Walt pointed you out at the pool."

"Yeah? What did my brother say?"

"Only that you had just come through a difficult divorce."

Diane's hard face cracked into a sardonic smile. "And thanks to my mother, I got full custody of the kids. She told the judge my ex beat them up. So now I have to raise them by myself while he swans about with his bimbo stripper in

Minnesota."

Unable to think of an appropriate response, Rex thrust the wine glass into Helen's hand and propelled her toward their door. "Walt is making dinner reservations for us. See you later, hen," he addressed Diane kindly, using the Scots term of endearment and whisking Helen into their suite.

"That Diane is hard work," she said when the door closed behind them.

A school counselor, she had an empathetic way of reaching out to people and a genuine desire to help with their problems. Consequently, she often attracted emotional and needy types. He feared Diane might be one of those people. And Helen could not resist helping them any more than he could resist trying to solve a murder.

"She's writing a novel based on her personal experiences," Helen informed him. "That's how we got on the subject of authors. It's a murder mystery."

"Can it be healthy to be writing aboot murder so soon after her parents' death?"

"She'd already started it. It's called *The Hollow Soul*, a literary work about—in her words—a woman's search to find herself after her useless, faithless, and callous husband abandons her and their children for a stripper from Minneapolis."

"Ouch. So she is drawing from actual experience."

"Many first novels are auto-biographical, she

told me. She's going through an extremely difficult divorce. I said the writing of her book could be therapeutic."

"Especially if she gets to kill him off?" Rex asked.

He groped about in his pocket for his pipe to enjoy on the balcony before they went out to dinner. His fingers encountered a small round object he had found across the street that morning before they learned of the dead bodies, and which he had forgotten about since then. "Let's hope it's a cathartic experience, like you said, and putting it down on paper prevents her from actually doing anything to her ex, even if he deserves it."

"So, where did you disappear to?" Helen asked.

"I was in the lounge talking to the other guests, a nice couple from Ohio, and a pair of college students from Florida."

He examined the embossed brass button while Helen sank on the bed and kicked off her sandals. "Did you find out anything new?" she asked.

"Only that someone's been leaving a calling card on the front door mat."

"What sort of calling card?"

"Dead cats."

Helen deposited her wine glass on the bedside table with a *thunk*. "I knew we shouldn't have stayed here," she muttered.

Rex helped himself to a small sherry from the

decanter on the dresser. "I'm sure it won't happen again. If it was a threat, the purpose for it has likely been served."

"You think the cats and murders are connected?"

Rex joined her on the bed and folded his hands beneath his head on the pillows. "If I knew that for certain, I could eliminate the guests. They've only been here a week, at most. The first cat appeared a month ago."

"Diane told me she's been living here six weeks."

"An ex-employee was terminated a week ago, but it's unlikely he planted the cats if he valued his job. If it had started after his firing, that would be a different matter."

Had Walt told the detectives about Taffy letting Raphael go? Perhaps not, if the man had been an undocumented worker. There were penalties in the States for employers who hired illegal immigrants. Rex thought if he could come up with a strong enough motive for murder, such as unjustified termination, to take to Captain Diaz without getting Walt into trouble, he might elicit some information in return; maybe find out what the autopsies had revealed. "And there's a guest who did a moonlight flit," he told Helen.

"Now that sounds suspicious."

"It does indeed."

Rex intended to get to the bottom of that

mystery as well.

# ~NINE~

That evening, they strolled to The Funky Parrot by way of Duval, whose storefront windows proved an unending source of fascination for Helen. The air was soft and balmy, puffy clouds obscuring the sun and providing temporary relief from the heat. Urban roosters with gleaming feathers clucked and crowed at every intersection, with a total disregard for the time or for the crowds milling about them.

Rex steered his fiancée out of the way of a satin-bodiced ballerina erratically pushing a stroller stocked with beer cans cooling in slush. Other remnants from Fantasy Fest clustered outside the noisy neon-signed bars, bare torsos displaying intricate designs, from spider webs to nautical themes, while a couple of girls minimally dressed as mermaids attracted their fair share of attention. On the street, carloads of youths yelled from rolled down windows above deafening bass amplifiers, eager to get an eyeful of flesh.

"I'm losing my sense of reality," Helen said.

"What is reality?"

"Now, Rex, don't get all philosophical on me. You know what I mean. There are so many oddballs in this place I'm beginning to feel abnormally normal."

A posse of motorcycles roared past the storefront façades and café terraces, chrome handlebars splayed high and wide, bleached-blonde women sporting tattoos seated pillion. Leading the pack was a man wearing a red-check bandanna, legs thrust forward on the pedals of a low-slung machine. The suntanned faces sped by, powerful arms steering the pulsating machines. It made Rex feel a shade wistful. If only he could feel as carefree.

"Happy you stayed?" he asked Helen when the growling Harleys had retreated far enough for him to be clearly heard.

"Did I have a choice?"

"Aye, and I hope you made the right one."

At that moment, he became aware of a pair of red stilettos striking the sidewalk ahead of them, their owner a tall brunette in a tight calf-length black skirt which impeded her progress. The impression was one of speed-walking. A scarlet silk scarf around her neck floated in the sultry air beneath her tumble of hair.

Helen tutted, following his line of vision. "Why, Rex, you old dog. I wonder… Is it a he or a she?"

"I think the new term for transvestite is a 'he-she.' " He had learned a whole new vocabulary from Campbell. "Gay" now meant silly. "Bad" had a positive connotation, as did "sick" and "insane." It was all rather confusing.

However, judging by the womanly cupped buttocks, he thought the person mincing ahead of them in the stilt heels had to be a she, but he didn't dare say so to Helen. In any case, he was spared further comment when, without warning, the brunette stepped into the street, hailed a bubblegum pink taxi with a flamingo on the roof, and hopped in the back in one fluid movement. The cab sprang forward and melted into the traffic.

"Wish I could attract a taxi that fast," Helen marveled. "Perhaps if I dressed as provocatively…"

A man in a Hawaiian shirt and chinos ducked into a second taxi cab. It screeched away from the curb and ran a red light at the next intersection.

"Did you see that?" Helen exclaimed in indignation. "The driver almost knocked down a pedestrian. I hope he gets a ticket."

"He won't. The passenger is a policeman."

"How do you know?"

"He was wearing plain black shoes with rubber

soles. He must be following that person."

"How exciting! I wish I could've taken a picture. Of all the memories I take away from Key West, the scene I'll probably remember most vividly is that creature in high heels jumping into a pink taxi and careening away. I wonder who he-she is."

Another mystery, thought Rex, and it was only day one.

By the time they reached the restaurant, Rex was ready for a beer. Even though the heat had lost much of its humidity, it was still warm, and his short-sleeved shirt was beginning to stick to his skin. Helen had developed a sheen on her nose, which she deftly blotted with powder from her compact while they waited to be seated.

As they were led to their table, Rex spotted Captain Diaz with a raven-haired beauty in a black halter-neck top. In intimate conversation at table, they made an attractive couple, and clearly would not wish to be disturbed. Rex tried to avoid eye contact, but his size and red hair were conspicuous under any circumstances, and Captain Diaz, noticing him, waved the new arrivals over to his table. The detective looked even fresher than this morning, dressed in a starched white shirt that set off his clean-cut dark looks.

"Please join us. We got the best table," he said. "And a four-top."

"Och, we couldn't possibly impose."

"We were just finishing dinner." Rex saw they were drinking coffee and sharing dessert. "This is my wife Rosa. Rosa, Mr. Rex Graves, from Scotland."

Rex completed the introductions. "My fiancée, Helen. Helen, Captain Dan Diaz of the Key West Police Department. You must think I keep turning up like a bad penny," he apologized to the detective.

Diaz smiled. "Key West is a small town, and the Funky Parrot is one of the best places to eat."

"Walt Dyer at the Dolphin Inn recommended it."

A steel band played a reggae pulse in a far corner by the bar, which hosted a lively crowd of patrons.

"It's hoppin', man," Diaz quipped. Rex guessed he was referring to the bar-restaurant's name. There was, however, no such tropical bird in sight.

A server pulled out chairs opposite the seated couple and added plates and silverware while the foursome exchanged pleasantries. Rosa, in a lilting accent, explained that her mother was watching the kids that night. Helen asked their ages. She adored children, but had none of her own, she explained ruefully—only the teenagers at her school, where she worked as a student counselor.

"Christian is ten and Maria seven."

"My, you don't look old enough to have a ten year-old!"

The women fell to discussing kids and became quite animated. Helen got on with everyone, which pleased Rex. The server set out menus in front of them.

"We had the Chilean Sea Bass," Rosa said as the newcomers perused their menus. "It was delicious. So is this key lime pie."

Rex ordered a Guinness and a Pinot Grigio for Helen, and then turned to Captain Diaz, who seemed relaxed after his meal, and more approachable than that morning. "Any progress in the case?" he inquired.

The detective shrugged. "Some."

"Hmm. An obvious clue left at the scene?" Rex asked hopefully, waggling his eyebrows in humorous fashion.

Diaz laughed. "If you mean a cigarette butt or a torn item of clothing—no. Sorry."

Rex produced the fake brass button wrapped in a clear plastic bag and held it to the light of the candle on the table.

The women paused in their conversation to look.

"What is it?" Rosa asked.

"Looks like a button off a costume," Diaz said. "Where did you find it?"

"Across the street from the Dolphin Inn, when we first passed by this morning and saw the patrol car parked outside. This was before we knew about the murders and people started arriving. We'd made an early start to get in as much sightseeing as possible before we had to re-board ship. The bodies must have just been discovered."

"It could be anybody's who participated in Fantasy Fest," Diaz said. "The Dolphin is three blocks from Duval."

"I picked it up out of curiosity. I wasn't acquainted with Fantasy Fest and the tradition of fancy dress at the time."

Diaz shrugged again, this time dismissively. "If it had been found in the alley, it might be of more interest."

"It was in between the street lights, in a dark spot facing the alley." Diaz continued to look doubtful. "Who knows? Its owner may have seen something," Rex said.

"We have no witnesses so far, in spite of a door-to-door and an appeal to the public."

"The button has blue thread attached." Rex shook the packet in enticement. "I forgot all aboot it until earlier this evening."

The detective nodded and smiled, reaching for the packet. "Thanks, I'll check it out."

"You came on a cruise?" Rosa asked Helen.

"We were supposed to go to Mexico," Helen said with a mock-reproachful stare at Rex.

"Where in Mexico?"

"Calicá."

"That's a nice port, but there's so much more to see in Key West."

Rex winked in gratitude at Rosa. The women then took off on the topic of vacations, interrupted only when the server arrived to take the food orders. Rex turned his attention back to Diaz. Although the detective had not appeared impressed by his discovery, he had been gracious about it. "Cause of death been established yet?" the Scotsman asked.

"We have the prelim results. No surprises. The Dyers succumbed to asphyxiation."

Rex felt sure that if something unusual had come up in the autopsy, the detective would not have told him, but he was grateful to have asphyxiation confirmed. "Chances are," he ventured, "the killer or killers forced the Dyers from the dark alley into the kitchen and suffocated them there. It would have been relatively quiet as long as they were threatened to cooperate."

"I agree. Less conspicuous hustling two live people into a building than transporting dead bodies to it, especially as the alley is not wide enough to accommodate a vehicle. The interior door leading to the main part of the bed-and-breakfast was locked, according to Walt Dyer, who arrived through the front door. His parents locked up every night before going to bed. They lived downstairs in a suite off the hall."

Rex remembered seeing a second door to the left on his way to the guest lounge. "Anything of interest in the suite?" he asked.

"Not as far as clues. A lot of clown paraphernalia. The walls of the bedroom and den are sherbet yellow. It's so glaring you have to wear sunglasses. And we found a cache of empty gin and vodka bottles in some pretty ingenious hiding places. Mostly cheap stuff, but a few of the square blue bottles too."

"Taffy Dyer must have been hiding the extent of her drinking from Merle if she went to such trouble," Rex remarked. "Her addiction is common knowledge among the guests. Hard to sustain a drinking habit on Bombay Sapphire unless you're well off."

"The Dyers were mortgaged up the wazoo."

Rex's and Helen's shared appetizer of conch fritters arrived, and Rosa tapped her husband's arm. The Diaz couple rose to leave.

"We'll have to do this again," the detective said, giving Rex a friendly slap on the shoulder. He kissed Helen on the cheek, and the women hugged.

Rex knew he would run into Diaz again at the bed-and-breakfast. As they departed, Helen remarked on what a nice couple they were, and how she looked forward to seeing Rosa again. The detective's wife had suggested they go shopping together, so she could show Helen the best stores.

After dinner, they strolled to Mallory Square to watch the street performers. Fire-eaters, acrobats, jugglers, and a slow-motion mime artist covered from head to foot in silver paint entertained the tourists beneath the array of stars. The multi-tiered *Fantasia*, which had dwarfed the dock, had long since set sail for Mexico, leaving a great empty space of dark water in its wake. On the horizon, a lit-up cruise liner pursued a southwesterly course to destinations unknown.

"Ships in the night. Romantic, isn't it?" Helen said with a sigh, hugging his arm.

"As long as I don't have to be on one," Rex replied.

He worried about getting seasick, though this was probably unlikely on such a large vessel. Still, he preferred *terra firma*. Expanses of deep sea made him nervous.

He secretly wished the *Fantasia* Godspeed and good riddance, and set his own course back to the Dolphin Inn where he felt sure a bigger adventure awaited.

## ~TEN~

They returned to the Dolphin Inn in good spirits, Helen by now happily resigned to their extended stay in Key West, or so Rex hoped. He used the main door key Walt had given them for access after eleven at night and entered the dimly lit foyer. As they went up the carpeted stairs, he heard voices coming from the hall to the guest lounge, and paused while Helen continued on up to their room.

"And the first thing I'll do is paint in here," Diane was exclaiming. "In fact, we need to change the color scheme of the whole place. What were they thinking!"

"It's my suite now," Walt answered peevishly. "I've been helping run the Dolphin since they opened it. You have no right to show up out of the blue and try and take over."

"Oh, listen to you! You never would have

dared raise your voice if *she* was still alive. And I need to be in here with the kids. They can't keep sleeping on cots. I can put bunk beds in this den."

"The suite's mine. And we can't afford to repaint right now. Anyhow, what are you gonna do to contribute? Your visit was supposed to be temporary, until you got back on your feet. It's been six weeks."

"You'll need help with them gone. We'll run the place together. We can do a better job of it. Merle was such a miser. Nasty cheap soap and recycled tea bags. No wonder repeat business was so bad."

Rex, who had paused on the steps to listen, continued up to his room, making a mental note to use the supply of tea bags he had brought with him for his trip. So, the younger Dyers would replace the elder Dyers, he ruminated, and the Dolphin Inn would live to see another day, perhaps in a different shade or hue.

"Rex, what were you doing?" asked Helen, who stood at the dressing table removing her earrings before the beveled mirror framed with carved walnut.

"Eavesdropping," he said.

"Shame on you."

"I know, but ever so interesting." He helped himself to a glass of sweet sherry from the decanter and went on the balcony overlooking the pool, illuminated a soft inviting blue. Gardenia, jasmine and white frangipani sweetly scented the air. Rocking back and forth in the wicker chair, he wondered which of the Dyers would prevail and move into the downstairs suite. He found himself rooting for Walt. He could not help but feel sorry for the prematurely middle-aged man. Diane, on the other hand, was as prickly as barbed wire. He made a mental note to handle with care.

"I'm finished in the bathroom," Helen called through the French doors ten minutes later.

Rex went to brush his teeth. It had been a long day since they docked early that morning. He left Helen to read her novel with the lamp on at her side of the bed and promptly fell asleep on the plush mattress, slipping at some point into a grotesquely vivid dream.

Cats the size of tigers chased a woman in red stilettos across the deck of a cruise ship rolling across a turbulent sea. Taxis whooshed down a water slide into a swimming pool, while a band of clowns alternately played clarinets and stuffed key lime pie into each other's faces. Suddenly, he awoke to a loud clang and sat bolt upright in bed. The sound had come from the alley. Helen stirred briefly, only to drift back off with a murmur of protest. She customarily took a pill when she traveled, unable to sleep well outside her own bed without one. Checking the clock, he saw it was past one in the morning.

He slipped into his sandals and, wrapping a

dressing gown over his pajama bottoms, exited the French doors to the balcony. It must have showered at some point in the night. The fronds of the coconut palms at the corner of the guest house dripped glistening drops, while crickets chirped a monotonous chorus in air still moist with the woodsy aroma of rain. Wind chimes tinkled faintly in the breeze. He peered over the balcony rail to where the fenced-off alley divided the Dolphin Inn from the adjacent property's back yard. Too dark to see anything. He looked below to where the inset lights of the kidney-shaped pool gave the water an ethereal blue glow.

Now that he was up, he decided to go and investigate. He left the suite and tackled the stairs, encountering no one. He opened the baize door off the hall leading into the dark passage to the kitchen, surprised to find both doors unlocked, and made his way across the linoleum by means of a night light over the countertop. The exterior door to the alley was locked and dead-bolted. He opened it and stepped outside. All was quiet.

A naked 40-watt bulb on the wall toward the back of the alley cast an orb of light where winged insects danced a crazy jig, leaving the surroundings in shadow. Across the passage loomed a garage wall of windowless brick. The warm air compressed within the boxed space held a putrid scent. A row of trash cans took shape as his eyes adjusted to the dark.

Among the covered PVC bins on wheels stood an old-fashioned refuse can, malodorous and missing its round lid. From its depths, a sudden raucous howl rang out, followed by a scraping of metal. Rex's heart jolted, his throat squeezed shut. In a state of paralysis, he waited for he knew not what.

A flash of white leaped out, claws extended over the rim. Fixing Rex with one green eye, the animal bolted in the direction of the street, black hindquarters blotted out in the night, white hind paws in retreat. Silence relapsed around him.

Luminous pale eggshells, discarded coffee filters, and fruit peelings littered the worn gray asphalt by the upturned lid. The ring of metal on concrete must have been what had woken him, though it was doubtful the cat could have dislodged such a heavy object.

Drooping yellow tape barred the alley entrance—hardly a deterrent to access. A car pounding a Hip-Hop beat passed in the street, gradually receding into the distance. Voices called out far away, a dog's bark echoed forlornly. Two jaundiced pools of lamplight spaced far apart spilled onto the sidewalk opposite the alley. A glance down the tree-lined street and again toward the back of the B & B, where Rex found the tall pool gate locked, satisfied him there was no one about. At least, not anymore.

# ~ELEVEN~

Rex was up again six hours later, surprised to see, when he returned to the alley from the street that the contents from the metal trash can had already been swept up, and the surrounding area disinfected with bleach, the distinctive acrid tang pervading the soft morning air.

He re-entered the yard by the white picket gate and, wandering back up the brick path toward the front door, paused beside a wooden bench to admire a bed of slender-stemmed bamboo orchids neatly tied to metal stakes. The yard contained a riot of flowers and bushes, and someone evidently spent a great deal of time tending the shrub borders stocked with pink begonia and saffron-flowered oleander. He leaned forward to inhale the heady fragrance.

"You take an interest in gardening, Mr. Graves?" asked a reedy voice behind him.

Startled, Rex turned to find the innkeeper staring at him through his thick lenses. "I'm trying to cultivate a garden at my retreat in the Highlands. The soil is poor, but azaleas and rhododendrons thrive there. Are those terrestrial orchids hard to grow?" He pointed toward the yellow-lipped, pale mauve blooms.

"They are quite delicate," Walt informed him, fussily shooing a bee off one of the erect stalks tied with yellow string. "They require a diet of well-rotted compost."

"What about pests?" Rex inquired.

"Pests? You mean aphids and spider mites?"

Walt's mind was on the orchids, whereas Rex wanted to know about the trash can. He maneuvered the conversation in that direction. "Any pests. Which reminds me: I heard a noise last night in the alley and found a cat pilfering in the rubbish."

"Cats used to be a problem in Key West before the authorities culled the population. Now it's roosters, which are protected." As if on cue, one crowed in the vicinity. "They're everywhere." Walt's gaze drifted to the street as a news van pulled up to the curb. He consulted his watch. "Early bird gets the worm," he said in the van's direction. "Are you ready for breakfast, Mr. Graves?"

Either he didn't know about the dead cats on the doorstep, which was highly unlikely, or else was choosing not to mention them. Not surprisingly, Rex concluded; they were not a subject guaranteed to welcome new guests.

He accompanied the innkeeper up the stone steps and into the foyer. Sunlight through the transom window illuminated the semi-circle of leaping dolphins, projecting a kaleidoscope of yellow, blue and green onto the smooth lilac wall. Crossing the threshold to the dining room, he saw he was the first guest to arrive for breakfast. Walt inquired whether he preferred cooked or continental.

"Cooked, please." Rex picked up copies of *The Citizen* and *Key West*, a weekly, from among the selection of crisply folded newspapers on the rack.

"Tea, coffee?"

"Tea, I think." He had forgotten to bring some of his own stock downstairs with him. He longed for a cup of robust black tea.

"Orange Pekoe or Earl Grey?"

"Darjeeling or English Breakfast?"

"No, sorry. The only other one I have is chamomile. I'll get you some English Breakfast from the store."

"Don't worry. Orange Pekoe will be fine. I just need a pot of water. Boiled, not micro-waved."

"Shaken, not stirred?"

Rex laughed at Walt's reference to James Bond. "I can always taste the difference. I'll brew the tea myself."

"Will your fiancée be joining you?"

"Later. She'll be having coffee and continental."

Rex requested whole wheat toast, his sole concession to a healthy diet while on vacation. In any case, he anticipated a lot of walking to mitigate any excesses. He and Helen planned to do a spot of sightseeing starting this morning.

The breakfast menu established, he headed toward a table by the bay window and selected a chair facing the door, giving him a cat-bird view of anyone who entered or exited the main entrance.

Unfolding the newspaper, he proceeded to read an account of the murders under the heading, *"Suspicious Deaths of Local Innkeepers."* A photo showed the Dyers at some function or other, Taffy an older version of her hard-faced daughter, with short, what could have been blond or gray, hair; Merle overall gray, desiccated, and rail-thin, unlike his son. He stood slightly back from his wife, with a deferential and mildly anxious look about him. Rex suspected he might have been the peace-keeper in the marriage. They presented an average and innocuous-seeming couple, with every expectation of many years still ahead of them. Too many years, in someone's cruel estimation.

Minutes later, Rex heard the thumping of cases on the stairs, and the Shumakers appeared in the doorway after leaving their luggage by the front desk. Chuck greeted him brightly.

"All packed and ready to go?" Rex asked.

"Back to Dayton," Alma replied with a rueful grimace. "After breakfast."

"Care to join me? My fiancée won't be down until eight."

The Shumakers readily accepted and parked themselves on chairs either side of him. Walt sidled over to their table with a tea pot containing steaming water for Rex. He took the Shumakers' order and promptly returned with a large urn and poured coffee into their mugs. He solicitously inquired whether they had taken their blue dolphin mug souvenirs, and appeared gratified to hear that they had.

"Anything in the paper?" Chuck asked Rex once Walt had left the room, eying *The Citizen* refolded on the table.

"Only what we already knew, except for mention of an article of clothing found close by the Dolphin Inn." Rex wondered if the reporter was referring to the brass button he had picked up across the street. Had Captain Diaz, thinking it of insignificant value in the case, thrown it out like a bone, to give the papers something to gnaw on while he pursued the investigation in another direction?

"What sort of clothing?" Mr. Shumaker inquired.

"Perhaps an item of fancy dress," Rex suggested, watching for a reaction.

Pirates wore bright buttons. What color had Chuck's pirate coat been? Blue to match the thread on the button, or black? Did Captain Morgan wear a black coat? Not that it mattered since, even if the button had fallen off Chuck's costume, he was staying at the Dolphin Inn and, therefore, any such evidence could not connect him conclusively to the murders.

Alma leaned back in her chair so she could see into the foyer, and whispered, "Wish we could stay longer and find out whodunit. But Chuck has to be back at work tomorrow for a walk-through."

"We have a home building business," her husband explained. "D'you think you could give us a call when you find out anything?"

Rex said he would be glad to.

"Peggy Barber said she Googled you and discovered you're a private detective." Alma's widely spaced eyes gleamed with excitement.

"Wait a minute! Who's doing the investigating here?" Rex joked, amused that Peggy had run a search on him. But then, being a writer, research would be second nature, he reasoned.

"Now we know why you were asking so many questions!" From his wallet, Chuck extracted a business card which read, "Shumaker Homes" in large letters, and handed it to him. "Call the cell number."

"Are you here to solve the case?" Alma asked, pouring cream into her coffee.

"Believe it or not, I just happened to be passing."

"But now that you're here..."

"Exactly." Rex and Alma exchanged knowing smiles.

"Anything suspicious so far?" she asked.

"Only a noise in the alley last night. Did you hear it?"

The Shumakers looked nonplussed. "What sort of noise?" Chuck asked.

"The clanging of a dustbin lid."

"You mean a trash can?" Alma shook her head. "Our room is on this side. We're in the Audubon Suite." She pointed to the ceiling directly above the dining room. "Did you go out and investigate?"

"Naturally, but I only saw a scrawny cat. I don't think it could have dislodged the heavy metal lid."

"It wasn't dead, was it?"

"No, it ran away."

Alma leaned forward. "Because, you know about the dead cats found on the doorstep?"

"Aye, Michelle mentioned it yesterday when we were all in the guest lounge."

"Very peculiar," Alma murmured, proceeding to sip her coffee. "So you think someone was out there?"

Walt brought in breakfast plates wafting tantalizing vapors of bacon and hot buttered toast, and refilled the coffee mugs before waddling off again in distraction.

"I can't help but wonder," Alma murmured, staring after him.

Chuck squirted ketchup on his pair of perfectly round fried eggs. "Maybe he'll dress up as his mother and stab some poor woman in the shower."

It seemed Walt Dyer, a character resembling the shy Norman Bates in *Psycho,* was the Shumakers' prime suspect in his parents' murders, though that didn't prevent them from attacking their breakfasts with gusto. As they were finishing, Helen arrived, freshly dressed in crisp white shorts and a pale blue T-shirt. She carried their straw hats and a canvas shoulder bag, and clearly meant sightseeing business.

"You must be Helen." Chuck hurriedly wiped his hands on his napkin and shook hers.

Alma beamed at her. "So nice to finally meet you. Shame we have to leave so soon. Especially with all the excitement. Rex has promised to call with updates."

Helen sat down with a cheerful smile. "I can't say I entirely share his enthusiasm for murder, but he is very good at solving them."

Walter, who had appeared with the coffee urn, spilled a few drops on the floral tablecloth as he was filling Helen's mug. He clucked an apology. "All finger and thumbs this morning," he lamented, mopping up the spillage with a spare napkin. He entreated Helen to help herself to the cereal, fruit and pastries on the buffet table and took himself off again.

Alma raised her meticulously plucked eyebrows at Rex. "A tad nervous, wouldn't you say? He spilled that coffee when he heard Helen say you were good at solving murders."

"He must be under a great deal of stress," Helen pointed out in her sensible way. "He just lost his parents and now he has to run this place on his own."

"A stroke of luck for him," Chuck opined. "You weren't here when Taffy and Merle were alive. At times you could cut the atmosphere with a knife." He downed the dregs of his coffee and stared at his watch. "Well, all good things must come to an end. Back to the grind." He pulled himself off the chair, his protruding stomach catching the edge of the table and threatening to spill the cream in the jug.

"Your taxi is here," Walt announced from the doorway.

The Shumakers took their leave, reminding Rex to call them in Dayton. Helen went to the buffet table while Rex watched them pile out the front door with their luggage, assisted by Walt. At that point the Barbers entered the dining room.

Divested of their pirate attire, they looked like everyday tourists. Rex introduced them to Helen.

"Well, Chuck and Alma certainly seem glad to get away," Peggy remarked as she sat down at a table with her husband.

"I got quite the contrary impression," Rex said. "Chuck could hardly tear himself away and was complaining that he had to get back to work and return to the cold weather in Ohio."

"Well, maybe they're just glad to have gotten away with *it*," Peggy emphasized with an enigmatic wink at Helen, who was returning from the buffet table with a bagel and a mound of green melon slices.

"My wife has a very creative mind," Dennis Barber remarked.

Most women did, Rex had noticed. All the same, he wondered what had prompted Peggy's suspicion of the Shumakers. A more ordinary and friendly couple you couldn't hope to meet. He made such an observation to Peggy, keeping his tone light-hearted.

"Appearances can be deceiving," was her response.

Rex readily admitted that one could not judge a book by its cover. On which subject, he recalled their novel showed a photo of the co-authors in black buccaneer jackets embellished with gold buttons, Dennis coiffed in the gold-braided tricorn hat he had with him prior to the book signing the previous day.

When Peggy seemed disinclined to elaborate on her comments regarding the Shumakers, Rex inquired about their signing, and she informed him it had been a success and they had autographed thirteen copies. Helen said she was looking forward to reading *The British Brigand* and thanked them for the dedication. She inquired whether there was any romance in the novel.

"Some, certainly. We try and appeal to a female readership as well. It's not all rape and pillage." Peggy described the hero to Helen as being loosely based on Admiral Sir Henry Morgan, a ruthless Welsh privateer who sailed the Caribbean in the seventeenth century, plundering the Spanish settlements and looting their gold. "In Panama City alone, he captured almost half a million pieces of eight," she informed her audience. "An absolute fortune."

And no doubt Morgan and his merry band had consigned thousands of Spaniards to their death in the process, Rex thought. However, greed did not appear to factor directly into the murders at the Dolphin Inn. The Dyers had been struggling to keep the bed-and-breakfast going, and there did not appear to have been anything of value worth killing for and risking the death penalty. Pirates had been hung for their sins three centuries ago. Florida used lethal injection. Someone or some persons had taken a huge risk for no obvious gain.

# ~TWELVE~

After breakfast, Rex and Helen made their way on foot past La Concha Hotel on Fleming and Duval, and south on Whitehead. The street accommodated grand clapboard homes and cottages in Caribbean pastels, small businesses, and low income apartment blocks, the sidewalks shaded by banyan and Royal Poinciana trees. After passing Bahama Village Market, they came to Hemingway's address located in the Old Town.

Behind a five-and-a-half-foot red brick and cement wall stood an unimposing but charming Spanish Colonial home built of limestone, with pale olive shutters flanking arched windows, and a veranda spanning the upper floor. Palm trees and lush foliage afforded additional privacy. Undeterred by the tourists and apparently quite at home, extra-toed cats stalked through the flowerbeds, lurked among the potted plants, and drank from the decorative tiled watering trough, a fixture from the men's room at Sloppy Joe's. Unlike the skeletal feline Rex had seen in the trash can the night before, these cats were well-fed.

"Aren't they adorable?" Helen said.

Rex thought some of them looked downright grumpy. The guide claimed they were descendants of Hemingway's pets, given him by a ship's captain. Apparently, this polydactyl breed was ensured a surer footing on rough seas. Rex suspected the guide was spinning a yarn. It was widely believed that Hemingway had not kept cats until moving to Cuba.

He had lived in this particular house throughout the 1930s with second wife Pauline Pfeifer, who had gone to the trouble and extravagance of having an outdoor swimming pool hewn out of the rock, the first pool to be built in Key West. Black-and-white photographs showed the literary icon in the company of big game spoils from hunting and fishing excursions in Africa and in the Gulf Stream. In the master bedroom, a ceramic cat statue, the replica of a gift from Pablo Picasso, graced a cabinet by one of the tall windows. Rex was beginning to detect a cat theme to his Key West trip. This was substantiated when he heard that an iron catwalk had led to Hemingway's book-lined study on the second story of the carriage house. Here, on a gate-leg table below a giant deer head, the author had worked on the final draft of *A Farewell to Arms* and pounded away at the typewriter keys in the creation of *For Whom the Bells Toll.*

It was all extremely fascinating, but Rex began to feel antsy. They had been at the museum for two hours. He wanted to get back to the Clown Case, as he now referred to it in his mind. Helen, sensing his impatience, led him out of the house and into the souvenir shop before they left. After a short browse, they selected a limited edition print, exotic and whimsical, of Hemingway's home by Bostonian artist Robert Kennedy, which they planned to put in Rex's converted hunting lodge in the Highlands to remind them of sunnier climes.

"Now we can go," she said after they had made their purchase and it was stowed in a bag.

"Stay if you like. I can take the picture back to the Dolphin Inn."

Helen hesitated. "Okay, I will, if you don't mind. I love this house. How lucky the Hemingways were to live here."

"I imagine Ernest wasn't always a lot of fun to live with. Didn't Diane say he was bipolar?"

Helen playfully pushed him on his way and told him she would rejoin him for lunch.

He wandered back to the guest house and went up to their room to drop off the print. The vase on the dresser had been refilled with a bunch of long-petaled yellowish flowers that exuded a fragrance so overpowering he went to open the French doors. From the balcony, he saw Diane Dyer reclining in a lounge chair by the pool, soaking up the rays, a cigarette dangling from her fingers. Michelle sat at the pool's edge, a fluorescent pink bikini skimpily covering her pale body, long legs submerged in the water. She too wore sunglasses, her dark hair bound in a ponytail.

"Well, of course, you can do what you want," Diane said in a cutting tone, the words carrying up to Rex on the balcony. "It's just that, under the circumstances, it's the least you could do."

"I didn't ask for it."

"You ungrateful little madam! Then what were you doing here? You could share that money with Walt and me, no? It's only fair." Rex strained to hear every word.

"You have the B and B," the student protested.

"Swap you, then. I know which I'd rather have."

Michelle kicked water off her foot. "I would stay, but Ryan wants to split."

"He's not family. You owe it to Taffy."

"When did you start caring about Taffy?" Michelle retorted.

"Listen to you. You're just like her! Selfish! You *should* go to her funeral. She was your great-aunt, after all. Plus, she left you a small fortune. God, I could strangle her." Diane stubbed out her cigarette and ground it vengefully into a metal ashtray on the concrete deck.

Rex wondered why Walt had omitted to mention Michelle's connection to the Dyer family when he was listing the guests the previous day. Nor had it come up in the conversation with the Shumakers and students in the guest lounge when they were all discussing the ex-owners. Presumably Alma had not known Michelle was Taffy's great-niece, or she would not have made those unflattering remarks about Mrs. Dyer in the girl's presence. In retrospect, Ryan had been tense and cautious...

Michelle got up from the pool and yanked her towel off an adjacent lounge chair. Shuffling into a pair of flip-flops, she said something to Diane he could not hear and flounced off toward the building, passing below his balcony.

He decided to go down for a chat with Diane and see what he could find out. Downstairs he bumped into Walt carrying a cardboard box in through the front door. An old red moped was parked by the white picket gate, a second box strapped with bungee cord to the back seat. A few spectators loitered on the sidewalk.

"Can I help you with that?" Rex offered.

"No, thanks. It's quite light. It contains my 'creatures of the night.'"

Rex's face must have shown his puzzlement.

"My moths," Walt explained.

"Ah. So, you're moving in?"

"Sure am. A few more trips and I'm done."

Walt made his way down the hall to his parents' old suite. Rex hastened to overtake him and opened the door to assist. A vision of yellow walls dazzled his eyes. He wondered how Walt had managed to wrest the suite from his sister's grasp, but, from everything Rex knew, the son had greater claim to it, having had to put up with his allegedly insufferable parents for longer. He continued down the hall to the guest lounge.

As he approached the pool, he said hello to Diane, who raised her sunglasses and squinted up at him, accentuating the lines spoking out from the corners of her eyes.

"Hi. I'm grabbing a break while the kids are at school. I suppose I should be helping Walt clean up the rest of the fingerprint dust, but I'm allergic to dust of every description." She brought the dark shutters back down over her eyes. "And mold and cat hair and pollen."

Rex availed himself of a lounge chair in the shade of the tiki bar. "How are things otherwise?" he asked.

She grimaced. "There's the funeral service to arrange, but who's gonna come?"

"None of the guests?"

"Well, Michelle might be attending."

"That's thoughtful of her," Rex said as though he had not overheard the women's conversation.

Diane responded with a *humph*. "She's Taffy's

long lost great-niece, if you must know. How precious is that?" she asked with arch sarcasm.

"Why did she keep her identity a secret? I was speaking to her yesterday aboot Mr. and Mrs. Dyer, and she never let on."

Diane gave a short, mirthless laugh. "Would you, if you were related? Her visit was news to me, too. She checked in under her boyfriend's name, Ford. She's Cuzzens. I didn't recognize her—hadn't seen her since she was a kid in braces. And Michelle isn't an unusual name in her age group. Her identity only came out when the cops questioned her. They came to me for verification. She said she told Taffy. I don't know why it was such a big secret."

"So she came to visit her great-aunt?"

Diane sucked hard on her cigarette. She nodded and jutted her chin on the out-breath, expelling smoke from both nostrils. "She's at college in Florida. She's second cousin to me and Walt. At least, I think that's right. I was never interested in doing a family tree. Taffy was always bragging to her sister about how wealthy she was and how she was going to leave Michelle a huge inheritance."

"Why would she do that?"

"Michelle lost her parents in a car accident, and was raised by my aunt Maggie. But the truth is, this place has a crippling mortgage, and business has fallen off in the past few years. My parents

104

were getting ready to sell and go back to Vermont."

Rex nodded, pondering the ramifications.

"They went up this summer looking for a place to retire. Merle missed the seasons. Walt and Raf were running the B and B, and it was doing good until Merle and Taffy came back. The guests didn't like my mother, and my bean counter father tried to skimp on stuff. Walt won't do that. He's got better business sense."

"So Michelle gets a share of the Dolphin Inn?" Rex asked, knowing more than he let on.

"Nope, equal split between Walt and me. Big whoop. But get this: Taffy and Merle each carried half a million dollars in life insurance policies. And guess who benefits?"

"Michelle?"

"You got it." Diane inhaled aggressively on her cigarette and spewed out a cloud of smoke. "And it's not as if she ever had to put up with them."

"Hardly seems fair," Rex sympathized.

"And me with two kids to support. I mean, you'd think Taffy could've left something to her grandchildren, whatever she thought of Walt and me. 'I am so disappointed in my children,' " she mimicked in a parody of her mother, which Rex guessed was probably not too wide off the mark.

"When did you know aboot the life insurance?" he asked. Had that been a factor in the murders?

"Yesterday afternoon when I spoke to the

family attorney." Diane jabbed the cigarette butt into the metal ashtray beside her lounge chair. "When I first mentioned it to Michelle, she acted as surprised as I was, said she wouldn't have to worry now about paying off her college loan. A million dollars! She could quit school and do whatever she wants. Her and her cute little boyfriend."

So, greed might be a motive, after all. Rex wondered if Detective Diaz was apprised of this development, but decided against asking Diane and coming off as too curious. He felt he was in a better position to elicit information from the residents of the B & B if they remained unaware of his semi-professional interest in the case. Only the Barbers knew, and the Shumakers, who had left town. Clearly, Diane needed someone to vent to, and he was more than willing to provide a sympathetic ear.

"I had to wait tables to pay for my degree. Taffy drank away my college fund."

"That must've been tough."

"I never invited them to the graduation. Figured they didn't deserve it, and Taffy might have embarrassed everybody by passing out."

"It cannot be easy having an alcoholic parent," Rex said, and meant it. If what Diane was telling him was true, she'd had a raw deal.

"That's not all." She fired up another cigarette. "Taffy suffered from NPD. Except that she didn't suffer from it—everyone around her did."

"Excuse me. NPD?"

"Narcissistic Personality Disorder."

"I see."

The English language was becoming increasingly abbreviated. Soon everybody would be talking in code. "Was this a clinical diagnosis?"

Diane almost choked on her cigarette. "Are you kidding? Taffy never sought help. She thought the sun shone out of her rear end. But I was there to witness her case history firsthand. She was a drama queen of the first order. Good drama or bad—it didn't matter as long as she was the center of it. Even though she would subtly provoke a scene, you'd always get blamed for starting it. And then she would cry crocodile tears and say how mean and crazy you were. She was happiest when other people were miserable. It took dozens of sessions with a therapist and thousands of dollars to finally figure out that my childhood was abnormal. In fact, I didn't have much of a childhood because she was the child. I also figured out that a lot of bad relationships in my life were not my fault."

Such a lot of anger and resentment, Rex thought. Was she truly over it? "Was your relationship with your dad any better?" he asked.

"He was complicit—weak and spineless. He enabled my mother's behavior. That makes him almost as bad."

Harsh words indeed. Rex dragged his lounge chair closer. His voice dropped to a conciliatory register. "Can't have been easy for him."

"He should've gotten Taffy help. Or left her if she refused it, instead of letting us kids suffer. If she'd left everything to me and Walt, I could be more forgiving," Diane said bitterly. "But even dead she continues to drag us into the vortex. And you see what a mess Walt is. He used to come home from school and she'd be half dressed, smashed out of her brain, and come on to his friends. He soon stopped bringing them to the house. I was the eldest and left home as soon as I could."

The diatribe, while exhausting Rex, seemed to have energized Diane.

"Well, your parents are gone now," he said gently. "You have two healthy kids and a chance at a new life. The circumstances may not be perfect, but it's up to you now."

She gazed at him in silence. He could barely make out her eyes through the dark lenses. She finally nodded reluctant agreement. "You're right, but I still think Michelle should cough up some of her windfall, help me and Walt out some."

"I saw Walt moving his belongings in," Rex said, realizing too late that Diane could not be pleased about it, if she knew.

"Yeah, well, that's a fight I couldn't win. Anyhow, it's best if me and the kids live someplace else."

Certainly for the guests, Rex thought. No more screaming kids in the pool.

"We're moving into Walt's efficiency until business picks up here and I can get something better. It's just down the street." She ground out her cigarette, less ferociously this time, and dragged herself off the lounge chair. "I should go help him. Thanks for the chat."

"You're welcome." He followed soon afterward. He was growing uncomfortably hot in his short sleeve shirt and had arranged to meet Helen for lunch. He felt in dire need of a cold beer.

He decided to go up to their room and freshen up. As he came out the guest lounge, he heard an ominous thump-thumping on the stairs. He stopped in his tracks. His first thought was that the spinster librarians had returned. Not exactly a heartwarming prospect.

## ~THIRTEEN~

As Rex reached the stairwell, the Barbers were on their way out, dressed in their pirate costumes and accompanied by a black wheeled carry-on case. It bulged to capacity, and Rex realized it was this article he had heard making its way down the carpeted steps, since it was evidently too heavy to carry. The Brimstone sisters were not back, after all, and he breathed a deep sigh of relief.

"You're leaving?" he asked the Barbers in surprise.

"We're headed for Pat Croce's Pirate Soul Museum for an informal signing outside," Peggy replied.

"We pedal our books at pirate venues," Dennis explained. "Sometimes we sell quite a few that way. It helps pay for bed and board when we winter in Florida."

"Occasionally we get asked to move on if the

museum or souvenir store is selling books on pirates and feels we're competing with their business," Peggy added. "But that doesn't happen very often. We just roll our books on to another location."

"Very enterprising," Rex said, thinking they were a respectable couple and added a touch of local color, so why should anyone care.

A pink flower consisting of five petals surrounding a five-pronged, red-striped corolla shaped like a trumpet was threaded through the eyehole of Peggy's bolero, to rakish effect.

"Oleander is highly toxic, Peggy," Rex warned her. "I don't know if you're aware. You don't want to be licking your fingers after touching that flower."

"Oh, I didn't know it was oleander. And I only thought white oleander was poisonous, probably because of the movie with Michelle Pfeiffer. It's so pretty I couldn't resist picking it from the yard."

"It goes nicely with the outfit," Rex complimented. "Just be careful."

"People sometimes stand us drinks on account of our costumes. And being a writer has its perks. Walt agreed to give us a special rate. Of course, Taffy tried to get us to pay full price when we checked in, but we said a deal was a deal, and we'd traveled from Kansas on a budget."

"It's not like the Dolphin Inn was full," Dennis

added. "She just liked to be the one in charge."

Rex wanted to ask Peggy about her earlier suspicions regarding the Shumakers, but Dennis was beginning to look impatient to be on their way. Nor did this seem the appropriate time or place. Walt squeezed past them in the foyer carrying empty boxes to the front door, which Dennis opened for him. Rex wished the Barbers good luck with their book selling and continued up the stairs to his room.

Helen joined him shortly thereafter, laden with bags. She must have gone shopping after leaving the Hemingway Home. She asked about his morning while she sorted through her purchases. He told her about his depressing conversation with Diane, and advised Helen to avoid her if she didn't want to spoil her holiday mood.

"Nothing could do that," Helen chirped. "I bought some postcards, which I'll have to write today or there'll be no hope of them arriving before we get home."

"It seems the young female student staying here is Taffy Dyer's great-niece," Rex informed her, preoccupied with the clown murders.

"Oh, yes?" Paying scant attention, Helen pulled a black cotton T-shirt dress out of plastic bag and held it up to herself in the dressing table mirror. "What do you think?"

"Nice," Rex answered. It looked like a long T-shirt to him, as in fact it was. "Diane told me

Michelle is the surviving beneficiary on a life insurance policy in her great-aunt's name," he continued. "And since there was one taken out on Merle too, and Michelle was, presumably, the second named beneficiary on that as well, the girl stands to come into a tidy sum."

"Well, there's your motive. I'm sure the cops will be all over it. So many murders involve life insurance policies it's surprising they're allowed." Helen went to hang the dress up in the free-standing closet made of distressed pine. "Too much temptation, if you ask me."

Rex sat on the edge of the bed. "A double murder is not that easy to accomplish in a small island town."

"Hard to dispose of the bodies, you mean?"

"Right. Perhaps the killer or killers thought they might as well leave them in the kitchen for all to admire."

"The sort of prankish thing two students might do?"

When Helen had finished sorting through her purchases, they set out for lunch and a spot more sightseeing, following a tour of attractions flagged on their street map. The weather continued its muggy vein of the morning, the sun intermittently peeking out beneath a wooly mantle of clouds, which sent pedestrians seeking the shade of trees and store awnings.

After visiting Ripley's Believe It or Not!, an

exhibit of weird and wonderful phenomena and oddities of every description, some of which did indeed defy belief, they spied the Barbers. Seated in full regalia at a table on the side of Sloppy Joe's fronting Duval, they appeared to have set up shop. Dennis wore his fake black beard, Peggy her seafaring garb of the seventeen hundreds. Rex recalled from his boyhood passion for pirates that there had been female vagabonds in britches sailing the high seas. A couple of tourists were just leaving the impromptu book signing, holding a copy of *The British Brigand*.

"Come and join us for a drink," Peggy called out when she saw Rex and Helen. "You look like you could use one."

"It is rather warm," Helen agreed, taking a seat beside Peggy and removing her straw hat. She ran fingers under her hair, fluffing up the dampened blond strands.

"The books are selling like hot cakes," Dennis said in his deep, somewhat theatrical voice, which went with the costume. The fake black beard disguised his weak chin better than his goatee, dramatically improving his looks.

"As long as we don't monopolize the table for long and drink something, the server doesn't appear to mind," Peggy said.

Rex asked the Barbers what they were drinking and ordered two ginger ales, a Guinness for himself, and one of the Hemingway specials for

Helen.

"Are you any female pirate in particular?" he asked Peggy.

"Oh, any of about ten of the most famous ones. Our costumes are a bit of a mish-mash."

"A dangerous occupation for a woman, I would have thought," Rex said, hoping he didn't sound sexist. "I mean, facing cannon balls and the depravities of a crew of cutthroats."

"Some women took to the life. For example, Anne Bonny from Ireland. It's a great story. She left her sailor husband for 'Calico Jack' Rackham, captain of the pirate sloop *Revenge*, and ultimately proved the braver of the two."

"How thrilling," Helen said. "What happened to her?"

"He was hanged, but she was spared on account of being with child. Some women followed their husbands and lovers to sea disguised as men, although it was strictly prohibited. The penalty in most cases, if caught, was death for the sailors who took women onboard."

The drinks arrived and Rex paid the tab. The loud country rock band finished their set on stage. Jimmy Buffet took over on the speakers, singing about wasting away in Margaritaville. Peggy took advantage of the reduced decibels to stand up and brandish a copy of their book in the air. "Signed copies of a popular pirate series while stocks last!"

she announced before sitting back down at table.

"Har-de-har," Dennis cheered in piratical fashion.

Clearly, Peggy was the driving force behind the writing duo, Dennis a willing accomplice. He seemed happy to let his wife do most of the talking. And yet his mind never appeared idle as his restless dark eyes roved about, taking everything in, on the lookout for Rex knew not what.

"I suppose pirates are a popular theme here because of the Captain Morgan Parade," Rex attempted to segue into the Shumakers and Peggy's suspicion of them. "The Shumakers told me they dressed up as pirates."

The Barbers sipped on their sodas, not taking the bait. Helen came to the rescue.

"Alma Shumaker has such beautiful natural curls, a lovely auburn colour. Just the right sort of hair for the times. She would have been referred to as comely, with her sweet, pretty face."

"She made a good pirate's wench," Dennis concurred. "Just the right figure for it, too. Hour glass, I think they would've called it in the olden days."

"Alma was very self-conscious about her generous hips," Peggy contributed, finally. "Though the tight shorts she insisted on wearing did nothing to help. It was incredibly tactless of Taffy to comment on her size in front of everybody when discussing her clown outfits. Poor Alma was in tears over it."

"I am sorry to hear that," Rex said with genuine sympathy. "I don't see the need to make hurtful and unhelpful comments."

"Taffy did it all the time," Peggy said. "And yet she couldn't take a slight herself. Chuck Shumaker, who wouldn't under normal circumstances say a mean word to anyone, defended his wife chivalrously and called Taffy a spiteful witch who couldn't hold her liquor. There was quite a scene. Taffy later apologized, but I don't think Alma ever forgave her. And I think it quite ruined her evening, if not her whole trip."

"Upset as Alma might have been, the insult hardly seems motive enough for murder, as you intimated earlier."

"But there's more to it than that, Rex."

Dennis shot his wife a warning look.

Peggy shrugged her narrow shoulders. "Motive? Maybe, maybe not," she told Rex. "But Chuck's a big guy, and getting the two frail Dyers tied up with Alma's help wouldn't have presented much of a problem. It was the perfect revenge for the humiliation, leaving them dead in their clown costumes, silenced forever with bags over their heads."

"My wife has a very fertile imagination. She dreams up most of the plots for our books. Mostly, I just edit."

Rex decided Peggy's version of events in the Dyers' kitchen probably required major revisions, but it had got him thinking about the psychology behind the murders. Peggy and Dennis continued to exchange meaningful glances. Rex, in turn, regarded the couple inquiringly. Peggy seemed eager to impart some further information, whereas Dennis appeared reluctant. Was it an act? Rex wondered whether husband or wife would prevail in this silent battle of wills.

"There's more," Peggy came out with at last, casting a look of apology at Dennis. "I think Rex should know since he's following the case. After all, we did tell the detectives about it."

Dennis did the sensible thing in the face of Peggy's determination to spill the beans. He complied, albeit with an irritated sigh of resignation.

"There was an even uglier scene between Taffy and Chuck after she insulted his wife," Peggy revealed. "He grabbed a clown figurine off the book shelf in the guest lounge and threw it down on the tile, where it broke into smithereens. Taffy let out a howl like you wouldn't believe. She said it was a priceless piece of china of great sentimental value, and if Chuck didn't give her two thousand dollars in compensation within twenty-four hours, she would call the cops. Chuck said, 'In your dreams.' Merle had to drag Taffy away, kicking and screaming. Walt went in to sweep up the broken pieces. He was excruciatingly apologetic."

Rex could imagine the scene as though he had witnessed it himself. Peggy had a gift for description.

"We heard the fracas and watched the whole thing from the doorway," Peggy added. "Chuck is such a gentle soul, as you know, but he was severely provoked."

"I didn't want you to get the wrong impression of Chuck," Dennis said, perhaps to explain his earlier reticence. "I probably would have reacted the same way in his situation. And no way that hideous piece of junk cost two big ones." He shook his fake black beard. "In any case, the Dyers can't sue now..."

"And when did this all take place?" Rex asked.

"The evening of the parade. At happy hour."

Except, it had not been so happy. Rex and Helen crossed amused glances.

"Yeah, it's funny to think about now," Dennis said. "That china clown smashing on the floor and all, but then the Dyers got murdered."

Rex wondered why Dennis felt it necessary to drive home the point. He felt quite capable of joining the dots himself.

At that moment, a male couple in shorts and sleeveless T-shirts entered the saloon and inquired about the authorship of the stack of books on the table. Excusing himself for reaching between

Helen and Rex, the older man of the couple picked up the top copy and turned it over in his hand. Rex glanced at Helen and, catching his meaning, she gathered up her shoulder bag, and they got up to leave, explaining to the Barbers they still had Harry Truman's Little Whitehouse to visit, and they would see them back at the B & B.

"Not a bad little earner if you're retired," Helen said as they exited the bar to the sound of Joe Cocker growling from the speakers.

"No, indeed, if pirates are your thing."

Rex wondered if perhaps the Barbers weren't a little too matey and hearty. With Dennis, it seemed a touch forced.

## ~FOURTEEN~

That night, after returning from dinner in the courtyard of a Thai restaurant on Greene Street, Rex sent Helen into the B & B ahead of him and said he would be up shortly. He wanted to take another look in the alley. It was dark, as on the preceding night, except for the bulb burning toward the back of the building. He ducked under the yellow crime tape. A shadow vacillated at the far end of the passage, an upright shape gaining definition and depth as Rex approached.

"Who's there?" he called out into the night.

"It's me, Mr. Graves," Walt's reedy voice responded.

Silhouetted against the light on the wall, the form concretized into that of the round-shouldered innkeeper holding a long object in his hand.

"Didn't mean to startle you," Rex apologized.

"After the disturbance last night, I thought I'd take a look." The trash cans appeared to be in order, the lid firmly in place on the round one. "Helen and I were just returning from dinner."

Walt asked where they had gone and, hearing the name of the restaurant, said he often got take-out from there. Rex felt he could not inquire what Walt was up to in his own alleyway. "Is everything okay?" he simply asked.

"I was moth watching." Walt waved a net attached to a pole. A moth hovered above him, outlined against a square of white sheet suspended below the light on the wall. Smaller insects nosedived into the bulb, glowing when they hit the target.

"Ah, I remember now. You're a lepidopterist."

"That one's a gypsy moth, *Lymantria dispar*, introduced to North America from Asia in the eighteen sixties. Most moths are nocturnal, but the male gypsy moth is also active in the daytime."

"Are you going to catch it?" Rex asked, taking pity on the harmless creature.

"Only if it had been a female. Those are white. I already have a moth." Walt bent down to pick up a lidded jam jar. Rex could see a dark shape fluttering inside. "A rare one. I'll show you my collection, if you like."

Rex decided it would be impolite to refuse and, in any case, he was curious to see inside the private suite. He followed his host round to the front door. Presumably the side door into the kitchen was bolted for the night as had been the case yesterday. Walt led Rex down the hall to his new living quarters.

"This used to be the dining room, which is now in the old front parlor," he explained. A marble fireplace, identical to the one in the dining room, had been converted to electric and embraced a pile of ceramic logs in the hearth. "The previous owners, Mr. and Mrs. Wurthers, did the remodeling, adding a wall here and there," he further explained.

A lamp beside the brown corduroy sofa blazed in a burnt-orange shade. The desk lamp on a computer-less workstation was likewise lit. Framed cases of dead moths lined the walls, the paint appearing mustard in the artificial light. The insects were, for the most part, drab in color, some furry, others resembling thick-bodied miniature airplanes, all mounted on pins, their pairs of feathery antennae pointing upward in $V$ formation.

"Here, let me put on the main light so you can see better," Walt said, following word with action. The walls changed to a fluorescent yellow. "There are over eleven thousand species in the world. Moths have existed a hundred million years longer than butterflies, and vary in a number of ways. For instance, most butterflies rest with their wings upright, moths with their wings spread flat."

Rex had never seen Walt so at ease. He evidently took pride in his collection and in his knowledge of these insects. Under the brighter lighting, Rex was able to make out tapestry patterns and tiger stripe highlights in gold and amber on the insects' wings. A more ornate showcase displayed a swallow tail specimen with delicate forewings and hind wings of transparent lime green.

"A luna moth from Florida," Walt informed him, standing by his side.

"It's exquisite." And dead, thought Rex, regarding its impaled body. The live moth in the jar could be heard making desperate attempts to escape, wings futilely tapping the concave glass.

Walt had placed the killing jar on the computer desk beside a pair of entomological forceps and a setting board, sharp pins at the ready. Rex wondered if an embalming process took place first.

"Is this all your stuff?" He looked about the small den where a couple of half unpacked storage boxes stood on the floor. The bedroom was separated by a pair of white wood louver doors folded back on themselves. A second door at the far end of the den opened onto a tiny bathroom. Rex glimpsed an outmoded pedestal sink in avocado and a translucent green shower curtain screening the tub.

Walt lifted his arms and let them drop back by

his sides. "Yup, this is it. I haven't accumulated much over the years, just a television and DVD player, and some books. And my moth collection. I cleared out the clown gewgaws to make a bit of space. Between you and me, they totally freaked me out."

Couldn't be more sinister than the rows of winged bugs, Rex bet; but to each his own. Poor Walt didn't have much to show for a man approaching forty. No photos of children, and none of his parents, either. Rex cast another glance over the small suite crammed with the most basic of furnishings. No sports trophies, no souvenirs from distant travels, no framed diplomas on the walls. Just the moth exhibit. The energy of the moth suffocating in the jar waned, its activities curtailed to mournful swoops in the confined space. The air in the room felt stifling, and Rex realized there were no visible windows. As if reading his mind, Walt reached for the pull on a ceiling fan, and a reviving breeze began to swirl.

"The cops took Taffy's computer away to search it for clues," the innkeeper said pointing to the desk taken over by the moth-collecting paraphernalia. "She ran her mouth on her Dolphin Doings blog, and they think she might have made enemies."

Rex did not personally subscribe to blogging and Tweeting, imagining streams of word particles polluting the information superhighway like so many fast food wrappers chucked out of car windows. He didn't know where people found the time. Of course, Campbell would deride his opinion as being "way" behind the times...

"Did Diane move out all right?" he asked as Walt set about aligning his framed moths with geometric precision.

"Oh, yes. She and the kids will be fine in my old place. It's not luxurious, exactly, but it's convenient, and it will do until we can find her something better. This way, we free up the Hemingway Suite next door to you. It's one of our best. Taffy never liked sacrificing it to Diane, but even she couldn't put her own daughter and two grandkids up in the attic. Not that there's anything wrong with the Writer's Garret or the Poet's Attic. Michelle and Ryan have the Garret. But those rooms are more cramped than our suites."

"Where was the Canadian businessman, Bill Reid, staying?" Rex asked. The newspapers said he was still wanted for questioning in connection with the murders. By the same token, it could be another red herring supplied by Detective Diaz, like the item of clothing. One couldn't let people think the police were making no headway in a murder case, Rex reflected, especially in a tourist town like Key West.

"He was in the McCullers', opposite you, the

one facing the street. It's a lovely suite done out in soft green fabric and mahogany wood."

"Any word from him yet?"

"Not a peep. I charged him for his entire stay, since he gave no notice of his intention to leave. Very suspicious his taking off like that without a word to anyone."

"What did he look like?" Rex asked. "In case I run into him in town."

"Regular sort of guy. Perhaps slightly below average height, thinish. About forty-five, maybe older? Graying hair—no facial hair that I recall. Always saw him in a suit."

Very helpful, thought Rex. Apart from the suit. He hadn't seen many of those in Key West. Walt, who had finished adjusting his picture frames to his satisfaction, asked if he would care for some herbal tea. Rex declined with thanks.

"Helen will be wondering where I got to. Oh, incidentally, which room are the Barbers in? Number four, or in the Poet's Attic?" Rex had never seen them leave or enter a room, and he wanted to be able to visualize where everyone was located.

"Number four, two along from you, overlooking the pool. We just renamed that suite The Jimmy Buffet, since he's writing novels now. We need to redecorate it in a more laid-back Florida style. It's where the Barbers stayed before, and they specifically requested that suite."

"They were here on a previous occasion?"

"Two years ago. I gave them a returning guest discount, like the chain hotels do with their rewards gimmicks. Taffy and Merle were against it, but it makes sense to me to get repeat business. Advertising is so expensive."

Rex wondered why the Barbers had failed to mention they had stayed at the Dolphin Inn before, when they told him about the "writer's discount." This contradicted what Walt had just said about giving them a reduced rate as returning guests. But perhaps it wasn't important, and the Barbers had simply wanted to give themselves airs as minor celebrities.

"Well, it's been nice chatting to you, Walt. Night, now."

Walt saw him out of his parents' old suite, and Rex headed upstairs, deep in thought. He could not see into the hearts and minds of the people he spoke to in his search for the truth. He had to trust to his judgment and instincts, sift through the lies and dissembling, see past resentments and prejudices, and all the delusions and pretense each person indulged in to one extent or the other. A rare being it was who was prepared to lay bare their soul.

"What kept you?" Helen asked from the four poster bed, where she sat propped up against a stack of pillows, a paperback open in her lap.

"Walt was showing me his moth collection."

Rex closed the door behind him and bolted it. "A pretty morbid hobby he's got going there, if you ask me."

"You mean, like solving murders?" Helen gave a soft chuckle.

"My victims are already dead. Walt traps the unsuspecting wee beggars in his catching net and crucifies them, and then puts them on display." Like the clowns.

"There's some rather gruesome stuff in this book as well." She held up her copy of *The British Brigand*. "Not to mention a lot of salty language. But it's quite entertaining, and it contains lots of interesting pirate factoids, such as what they did about personal hygiene."

"I didn't know they had any," Rex remarked on his way to the bathroom to prepare for bed. He waved his toothbrush through the door. "I bet they didn't use these. That's why they had so many gold teeth!"

"I'd rather have you than a pirate any day," Helen responded from the four-poster.

"You can have me in aboot five minutes, me darlin'," Rex announced in deplorable imitation of a ribald pirate.

After all, he couldn't be thinking about murder all the time.

# ~FIFTEEN~

Entering the dining room the following morning, Rex was surprised to see the two students seated at breakfast toward the back of the room. Heads bent over the table in animated conversation, they broke apart when they spotted him, and fell silent as he took his usual place by the bay window.

"You're up bright and early," he remarked with good cheer.

They smiled back politely. Rex got the distinct impression he had interrupted something important. He decided to let them be, knowing from experience that young people were often not at their best in the morning. He wished he could speak to Michelle alone. However, that might prove difficult. She and Ryan were like conjoined twins; wherever one went, there went the other.

Walt bustled in soon after Rex was seated. "We have grits on the menu this morning," he informed his guest with some measure of pride.

Rex had partaken of grits on a previous trip to the States and had not been unduly impressed. Perhaps he had needed to season it liberally with something, but had not been sure what, and had experimented with various condiments to no avail. In this instance, he declined and settled contentedly for Walt's inimitable scrambled eggs, sausage patties, and fried toast. Just as well Helen wasn't around to see him consume it. She was going to take it easy after their sightseeing stint the day before, sleeping in this morning and then relaxing by the pool.

As he shook out his copy of *The Citizen,* he saw on the front bottom half of the page that a man was being held for questioning in the Dolphin Inn murders. His heart quickened. Was this the elusive Bill Reid, or somebody else? It appeared Captain Diaz and his team were making greater inroads into the case than he was, not surprisingly, given their resources. All he had was one set of eyes and ears—and the advantage of being *in situ.* This morning he resolved to use his feet and get a bit of legwork in before lunch. He peeked through the gauze drapes.

"Fewer people nosing about outside today," Ryan remarked from across the room, finally opening up the conversation.

"All to the good," Rex replied. "I suppose interest is already dying down."

"That's because they were a couple of old people. If it had been a beautiful young female that was murdered, the coverage would never stop."

"You may have a point," Rex conceded. "All the same, the Dyers weren't *that* old." Though it probably seemed so to a twenty-something. "Someone mentioned you were Taffy's great-niece, Michelle," he said, with Walt out of the room. Nothing ventured, nothing gained, he decided.

A telling pause ensued. Rex waited.

"Yeah, but it's not like we were close," Michelle finally replied, emphasizing the word "close" and squirming in her chair. "I mean, I knew her when I was a kid, but then she and Merle moved here to open up this place, and I never saw them again—until now."

"Yet they remembered you in their will, so to speak."

"News travels fast," Ryan said.

Rex could detect across the intervening distance an expression of irritation. He might as well have told Rex to mind his own business.

Rex winked at him. "B and B stands for Busy Body, didn't you know?" Ryan relented and rewarded him with a lucent grin. "People are invariably curious regarding their fellow travellers," the Scotsman went on. "The cosy nature of bed-and-breakfasts promotes neighbourly interest, even gossip. It goes with the territory. Hotels tend to be more impersonal."

"We usually stay in hostels. But seeing as how Chelle's relatives ran a bed-and-breakfast and she was in Florida, she felt she should see them..." Ryan tailed off in evident discomfort.

"Taffy and Merle must have been delighted to renew your acquaintance, Michelle." Rex feigned interest in his newspaper, turning a page to a story concerning the biggest marlin ever caught in the Keys, and described by the writer as "epic." He decided to save it for Campbell, an avid fisherman.

"It was Ryan's idea," Michelle responded. "I guess Taffy felt guilty not raising me when I was orphaned, but she already had two kids of her own, and I don't think she would have been considered a fit guardian anyway."

Walt waddled in at that moment with a pot of water for Rex's tea. "Sorry it took so long. A watched saucepan never boils, or whatever. But I know you don't like it done in the microwave. Breakfast is coming up."

Rex poured the hot water into a mug and dangled his English Breakfast tea bag in it, looking forward to the reviving and refreshing brew.

"Anything else for you guys?" Walt asked the young couple.

"Thanks, but there's someplace we gotta be,"

Ryan said.

Rex noted then that the student was wearing a pressed shirt and Michelle a pink blouse.

"And I need to buy a black dress," she said. "Should we send a wreath to the funeral home? Not sure how all that stuff works. I've only ever been to memorial services, apart from my parents' funeral, and I don't remember much about that."

"Michelle, I'm so sorry. How dreadful for you." Walt genuinely seemed more concerned about her loss than his own. Rex felt there might be hope for some bonding among the Dyer family, after all. "Don't worry about flowers or anything," he assured her. "We're getting them from the front yard."

The young couple got up to leave, and Rex bid them good day. Michelle was a tall girl, the same height as Ryan in low heels. He heard the chime of the front door and watched them hurry down the path. Where were they were off to so early? Rather early for dress shopping, he mused. Walt left the room and promptly returned with his plate of food.

As Rex ate and perused the other news of the day, he told himself he shouldn't let the fact that Ryan reminded him of his son cloud his judgment in any way. After all, the students had a lot to gain from the elder Dyers' deaths. Taffy had made no secret about leaving money to her great-niece, and had even boasted about it. For all he knew, Ryan could be a callow young fortune hunter preying upon Michelle's vulnerability. Losing both her parents in a car accident when she was a young and, by all accounts, only child, could not have been easy.

Rex felt a wave of sadness and regret. A drunk driver had taken his father when he was a small boy, and his son's mother had succumbed to breast cancer when Campbell was fifteen, so Rex knew something about the loss of a parent—or so he had thought until he met Walt and Diane Dyer.

Dabbing at his mouth with the floral cotton napkin provided, he rose in turn and from the buffet table set a mug of coffee, a bowl of cubed watermelon, and a mango muffin on a tray for Helen, which he proceeded to take upstairs.

Depositing it on the bed beside her, he gave her sleepy face a kiss. "Wakey, wakey," he said.

"Mmm, breakfast in bed. How wonderful." She sat up and stretched.

Rex went to pull back the drapes and let in the morning air through the balcony doors. A large yellow butterfly fluttered outside and alighted on the glass pane. He shooed it away to discourage it from entering the room and becoming trapped like the doomed moth in Walt's jar.

"Where are you going?" Helen asked as he patted down the pockets of his lightweight pants, checking he had his wallet, room key, and sunglasses.

"The police station."

"A break in the case?"

"Not sure, but I may have an excuse to see Captain Diaz, and perhaps I can learn of any progress at his end."

"The murders don't seem real, somehow," Helen said drowsily, stirring her coffee. "Perhaps because I didn't see the bodies and they were dressed as clowns, which, forgive me for saying, sort of gives it a more cheerful aspect."

*You didn't see the clowns*, was what went through his head in response.

"Of course, I know that's nonsense. I mean, murder is murder." She nibbled on her mango muffin, moist crumbs tumbling onto the tray.

"Sorry to be running out on you. Will you be okay?"

"Don't worry about me. If I finish the pirate book, I'll start the Carl Hiaasen novel you'll never have time to read."

"Right-oh." *And make sure you bolt the door if you take a shower*, he almost added, thinking of Walt and his creepy moths. However, he didn't want to scare her. He blew her a kiss on his way out of the room, locking it after him, even though their host had a key.

Once on the street, he turned left, map in hand, making for the Key West Police Station, having first referred to the business card that Captain Diaz had given him. He decided to walk the moderate distance unless he became too hot or footsore on the way. A Conch Tour Train clanged its bell in a nearby street, the words of the animated driver-guide reduced to a burble. From the opposite direction an electric golf cart zipped by, driven by a youth barely old enough to have a permit, egged on by three drunken and equally youthful companions. It swerved close to the curb by his feet, eliciting a chorus of whoops and cheers before continuing its meandering course toward Duval Street.

He continued to follow the sidewalk eastward and turned onto Frances, a peaceful residential street festooned with palms and flowering trees. Strolling along, he gazed into mature gardens chock-full of colorful native plants and exotics. A ways down, he noticed a vine-ridden guest house boasting, in the lushly overgrown yard, a spreading banyan tree, which gave its name to the establishment on a carved piece of driftwood nailed to the trunk. The Banyan Inn was more to Rex's taste than his cutesy B & B, in spite of the telltale signs of neglect.

Temporarily distracted by the scenery, his thoughts reverted to Michelle Cuzzens' possible involvement in the case, she being the main beneficiary in her great-aunt's murder—times two, since Merle Dyer had died with her. Why had she arrived incognito, booking in under her boyfriend's name when they were not married?

Rex had seen in the register that Ryan's last name was Ford, and Diane had confirmed as much.

Rex didn't see Michelle acting alone. Quite possibly she and Ryan were in it together. For one thing, the red lacquered extensions on her nails had been perfectly intact when he first met her, the day after the float parade. He could not see her tying up the practiced knots around the victims' wrists and throats, even if she had had time to get her nails repaired. Ryan hailed from Ft. Lauderdale and had probably spent time on the water. Interestingly, the students had not given their college address in Gainesville.

It was possible Michelle saw Ryan as her knight in shining armor and been persuaded to commit the crime in pursuit of financial gain. And yet she was not the only person in the family with a motive. According to Diane, Taffy had told lies about her daughter's ex to get him limited visitation with the children, which put her daughter in a bind, since Diane now had Justin and Kylie full-time. Not that Mrs. Dyer had shown her only grandchildren much affection, by all accounts. She had resented their taking up space at the bed-and-breakfast. Obviously, not much love had been lost between mother and daughter.

Spiteful by nature, it seemed, Taffy had fired the popular and diligent Raphael. She had refused him severance pay and had threatened to report him to Immigration Services if he made trouble. That had been Walt's version of the facts. It could be a problem finding the ex-employee, however; akin to finding the proverbial needle in a six square-mile radius comprising twenty-five thousand full-time residents—a haystack swollen by over two million visitors each year. These statistics Rex had read somewhere and retained.

Approaching the corner of Angela Street, he spotted a black-and-white cat with a stiff gait skirting the sidewalk. In spite of its lightening-flash departure at their first encounter, he recognized it as being the same animal he had seen in the alley. Its markings closely resembled a tuxedo, snowy dress shirt and spats, giving the feline a dignified aspect, as of an elderly member of a gentleman's club.

"Hello, old fellow," Rex called softly.

It paused briefly, lifting its grizzled muzzle to gaze with one eye in his direction before slinking off into the grounds of the city cemetery, where it disappeared between the black railings into the undergrowth fringing the tombs and headstones. The graveyard lay two blocks from the Dolphin Inn, quite a trek for an aged cat-about-town, Rex reflected.

Would the Dyers find their final resting place in this tranquil spot? Could their spirits ever find peace while the killer or killers went free? Taffy and Merle had not won rave reviews from the people Rex had spoken to, and yet he felt he would not find rest either until their murders were solved.

## ~SIXTEEN~

All the way east on Truman and almost hidden away to his right on North Roosevelt Boulevard, Rex finally found the Key West Police Station, a modern facility whose generous parking was sprinkled with blue-on-white patrol cars. A circular two-story atrium housing a tiled fountain led to the entrance. A notice encased in glass directed Rex to the appropriate floor.

At the information window leaned a Hells Angel wearing a red-check cotton bandanna and holding a terrified youth by the scruff of the neck at the end of an arm sleeved with tattoos. His other hand gripped a soft leather bag with a profusion of buckles and straps.

"He snatched this purse," the biker explained to the desk sergeant, a heavyset man with dark patches under the arms of his short black sleeves.

"So we collared him." This from another biker

who stood off to the side, and whose round helmet and rotund frame reminded Rex of Sergeant Shultz from *Hogan's Heroes.*

"Your name, sir?" the cop asked the first biker.

"Twisted Angel."

"And yours?"

"Rollin' Roy."

"Domicile?"

"Houseboat Row. It's his crib." Rollin' Roy jerked his helmet at his friend.

"Houseboat got a number?"

Rollin' Roy gave a description of a psychedelic houseboat and provided its location relative to the other floating homes, adding that the cop could not fail to miss it.

The desk sergeant gave a heartfelt sigh. "You expect me to write all that down?"

"The boat's called 'Tangerine Dream,' " Twisted Angel said. "Don't recall a number. You gonna book this douchebag?" The tall biker handed over the silvery sheened purse in evidence. "He was fleeing the scene."

The hangdog youth, his mouth marred by ulcerating sores, wore a drugged expression and dared not move a muscle and risk antagonizing his formidable captor.

The sergeant thanked the bikers for their community service and waved over an officer. He then turned to Rex. "Can I help you?"

"I've come to see Captain Diaz of the Criminal

Investigations Bureau."

"You got an appointment?"

"Not specifically, but I think I may be able to help in the Dolphin Inn murders."

The sergeant raised black caterpillar eyebrows and cast a glance over his respectable clothes. For Key West, Rex felt almost overdressed. "One minute," the cop said, reaching for his desk phone.

Twisted Angel, divested of his prey, approached Rex. Of comparable size, they stood eye to eye. The similarity ended there. The biker resembled a mature and weathered Jeff Bridges, graying blond hair windblown beneath the confines of the red-check bandanna. "You got something on the killer?" he asked, squinting through crystal gray eyes.

Was the man threatening him? "What if I have?" Rex asked.

Twisted Angel's mouth relaxed into a grin amid the graying stubble. "Nothin'. Just that the son, Walt, did my niece a good turn. I hope he finds out who snuffed out his folks."

Rex's mind leaped back to Michelle Cuzzens. "What is your niece's name?"

"Rihanna."

"I'm staying at his bed-and-breakfast. I have to admit, I never associated Walt with good deeds, *per se*." At least, not in the moth department.

"He gave Rihanna money when she needed it.

And he's helped the other girls out."

"What other girls?" Rex asked in further surprise.

"Those working at the House of the Rising Sun. I got my niece outta there soon as I found out."

"The House of the—"

The desk sergeant interrupted with, "The captain will see you." Meanwhile, Twisted Angel's stunted friend grabbed the biker's muscle-bound arm and told him they had to get rolling.

"See you around," Twisted Angel said as they left.

The words gave Rex pause, but only briefly, directed as he was through a swing door leading into a corridor. Another door opened onto a dozen populated desks ringing with phones and supporting incandescent computer screens. Walls displayed magnified street maps, whiteboards and notice boards. The air was redolent of fried food, Old Spice aftershave, perspiration, and printer ink. Sealed windows preserved the odors along with the air conditioning.

At the end of the hall, he found the captain in a glass-walled office, seated behind a desk with his back to a view of the parking lot.

Desk phone to his ear, Diaz pointed Rex to a chair. "You gotta be kidding," he was saying into the receiver. "Well, get another tail on her. Ask around. Bars, stores, cafés. Somebody got to

144

remember a broad with a bod like a forties pin-up. Find out who she was seeing. Don't seem natural a gorgeous brunette was in Key West by herself."

Clean-shaven in a starched white shirt, the detective dropped the handset into the cradle. A welcoming breeze spiraled down from a propeller fan whirring above their heads. A portrait photo of the detective, his wife, and two elementary school-age children took pride of place on a credenza.

"What you got, Mr. Graves?" he asked, clasping his hands together on the cluttered desk, his fingers tipped with short, square nails and adorned by a gold wedding band. "Manage to shake anything loose?"

"I've spoken with everyone staying at the Dolphin Inn. I understand there was a guest, a Mr. Bill Reid, who left suddenly."

"We finally tracked him down and cleared him. He said he left the night of the murders because he couldn't take another day of Taffy Dyer butting into his business. He checked into the Hampton Inn. First he knew about what happened was when he read the paper."

"You believe him?"

Diaz twiddled a yellow pencil between his fingers. "We ran a background check, spoke with some of his associates. He's here from Toronto on legitimate business. He didn't come forward because he didn't want to get mixed up in the

145

murders, and claims he was packed and out of the bed-and-breakfast by nine on Saturday night."

"The woman you were discussing on the phone just now... I saw someone fitting her description yesterday evening."

"Yeah?"

"Tall brunette, red silk scarf. She took off on Duval in a pink taxi with a flamingo on the roof."

"Flamingo Cabs. My sergeant was following her."

"Who is she?"

"Connie Lamont, thirty-six. And anything I tell you is in strictest confidence, okay?"

Rex nodded solemnly.

"I checked you out, Mr. Graves. And I'm talking to you because you solved the student case up in Jacksonville, which the cops seemed unwilling to pursue."

Rex felt most gratified to hear this. "I'll help in any way I can. And I'm the soul of discretion. So, what else can you tell me about Connie Lamont, detective?"

"She works for an insurance company in Fort Lauderdale. Their human resources department told us she took two weeks' vacation time. We picked her up on Truman and interviewed her, but she refused to say why she was in town and where she was staying. Told us to mind our own business and that she'd sue the police department for harassment if we didn't keep off her case. Real nasty mouth on her."

"Is she a suspect?" Rex asked, curious about the coincidence that Ms. Lamont came from Ryan's home town.

"She was seen by a neighbor in the vicinity of the B and B around the time of the murders. He thought she might be a pro that time of night or dressed up as one, and was able to give a detailed description. Now, unless there's something else, Mr. Graves? If I don't wrap this double homicide up, like yesterday, the county boys will be all over us city cops like skeeters on snowbirds."

"Sounds like a turf war," Rex prodded, sensing this was a point of contention with the detective, and anxious to keep the conversation going to find out more about the case.

"You may have noticed my ethnicity," Diaz said. "My family sailed over from Cuba when the cigar-rolling business was booming in Key West. We been here for generations, though most of my family has since moved to Tampa. I'm a regular Conch."

"I take it that's jargon for a Key West local. I envy you. I like the relaxed feel of this place."

"It used to be more exotic. Now it's as touristy as a spritzed down margarita. Thing is, I can't imagine being someplace else."

"You seem very young for a man in your position," Rex flattered him in all sincerity.

"Lucked out. Got promoted for busting a local

drug cartel smuggling marijuana out of South America. It put a lot of noses out of joint, both inside and out of law enforcement." Diaz gave a wry grimace, as Rex laughed at his play on words. "I'd sure like to nail this double homicide," the detective concluded.

"Have you pursued the inheritance lead? Michelle stands to come into a considerable amount of money. Motive, means, opportunity..."

"Yeah, all of the above," Diaz agreed. "Had her and her boyfriend come in earlier today. Interviewed them separately, and their alibis appear to hold up. Thing is, anyone off the street could have taken the Dyers' key off of them and dumped their bodies in the kitchen. Same with the household items used to suffocate and tie them up. The rope and plastic bags could've come from under the sink, or just about anywhere."

"The same rope was used to secure Walt Dyer's orchids to stakes in the flower bed."

"You noticed."

"What did the autopsy report reveal beyond cause of death?" Rex asked.

"A high level of alcohol in both victims, which isn't surprising at Fantasy Fest. And Taffy Dyer was an alcoholic. The state of her liver proves it."

"A lot easier to subdue them if they were intoxicated, especially if they were threatened with a weapon. I don't suppose one was found?"

"We should be so lucky. Probably Merle Dyer

was suffocated first, since he posed the greater physical threat—as far as an unfit guy in his sixties can pose any kind of threat. Kinda deaf too, from what I heard. But that could've been a convenient case of selective hearing, to tune his wife out. Merle still had his wallet on him, not that there was much cash, and Taffy all her jewelry."

"Did the Dyers always dress up for Fantasy Fest?" Rex inquired.

"Apparently. Walt said his mother had a thing for clowns."

"I wouldn't be caught dead in a clown's costume," Rex said with a sardonic smile. "Seems like a very cruel joke on someone's part. Methodical killing, but with all the appearance of malice."

Diaz shot him a keen look. "You got any ideas who?"

"Someone who knew the Dyers well and held a deep-seated resentment. Did Michelle Cuzzens mention the dead cats on the doorstep?"

"Yeah, we did find a dead one in the trash. Oleander poisoning. Walt Dyer denies knowledge of how they got there."

Rex sat back in his chair. "Less than one leaf of nerium oleander would be required to kill a cat." The elongated dark green leaves were highly toxic. In fact, ingestion of any part of the plant could cause gastrointestinal and cardiac effects in humans and animals, he recalled, consulting his encyclopedic memory.

"We found crushed leaves in the metal trash can Walt Dyer uses for compost. He grows oleander in his yard."

"I know, but it's a pretty prolific plant in Florida, isn't it? I've seen it in medians on interstates." An evergreen shrub in the dogbane family, the star-shaped flowers in white, red, pink, salmon and yellow formed attractive screening. "I startled a cat in the rubbish the other night. A black-and-white creature with one eye."

"That would be Willie's cat, a regular Dumpster diver, that one. Willie's a local bum. Wears a blue coat in all weather."

A blue coat, Rex registered. "If that's his neck of the woods, he just might have seen something the night of the murders."

"I don't know where we'd find him." Diaz pensively rubbed his clean-shaven jaw. "Used to see him panhandling with his cat on Duval. Not recently though. The cat goes by Mac, or else Pirate or Nelson, on account of his missing an eye. He has several aliases." The detective smiled and shook his head. "You gotta love this place."

"Is Willie approachable?"

"You mean clean? Yeah, clean enough as transients go. Pretty scary looking, but harmless."

"I meant would he talk to me?"

"Willie is more likely to *converse* with you. If you can locate him, he's partial to hard candy, which might account for why he has no teeth. But, like I said, he might've moved on."

The desk phone blurted a beep. "Put her on." Diaz proceeded to speak in dulcet Spanish, presumably to Rosa, nodding briefly and apologetically to Rex and making him understand the meeting was over.

Rising from his chair, Rex stuck his hand up in a salute of thanks and farewell, and left, not in the least disappointed by his visit. Captain Diaz had been gracious and accommodating with his time. And had placed his trust in him. Rex only wished he himself had had more to offer, a situation he meant to rectify forthwith. He hoped the vagrant had not disappeared.

## ~SEVENTEEN~

Once outside the police station, Rex walked a short distance before finding a convenience store, and thereafter took a cab back to the cemetery. He approached the spot where he had seen Willie's cat disappear between the railings. According to his street map, supplied on behalf of The World Famous Conch Tour Train, the cemetery covered an area of four blocks in the center of town, hemmed in by Frances, Angela, and Olivia Street, and Windsor Lane, showing the main entrance on Angela. He had little hope of finding Willie here or anywhere else, but the gravesite beckoned with its stillness and spots of shade after the oppressive mid-morning heat.

He followed a leafy lane running alongside the cemetery railings until he came to a pair of white pillars flanking an iron gate. A sign inside the entrance informed the public that the nineteen-acre graveyard dated from 1847 and commemorated Americans and Cubans who had died for their homelands. Crossing the cemetery in the direction the old cat had taken, Rex passed palm groves, crowded tombstones, and religious statues. Family plots containing above-ground granite vaults enclosed by rusty iron grille-work followed in secluded succession. Urns and vases held flowers wilting in the sun or bouquets made of material grown discolored and dusty. Cracked asphalt paths and sandy trails led him deeper among bushy flowering trees and crumbling cement crypts overrun by green iguanas.

At length, in a quiet and neglected corner, he came across a low monument in the shape of a table. Beside it lay a pile of flattened cardboard and sheets of corrugated iron. Willie's feline friend sat on the carved stone surface judiciously licking a paw after a repast of tuna from a dented can. On the grass, a hardback book, battered and watermarked, and a brown paper bag twisted at the top, which Rex suspected concealed a bottle of spirits, confirmed human habitation.

"Where's your master?" he inquired softly of the cat, maintaining a few yards between them in order not to scare it off its perch on the slab.

Paw held aloft in front of its grizzled muzzle, the cat suspended its ablutions and stared at him for a moment through its remaining green eye. Then, growing aware of a rhythmic scraping sound as of a shovel digging in earth, Rex went to investigate the source.

The scene that met his gaze seconds later surprised him, in spite of Captain Diaz's words that might have prepared him better. A man not much shorter than Rex leaned in repose against the trunk of a shade tree, the wooden handle of a shovel in the grip of massive knuckles. A squirrel-red bush of a beard, such as worn by soldiers in the Civil war, contrasted starkly with the blue of the brass-buttoned felt coat, which resembled a reject from a costume store. Even though the garment was of light material, Rex wondered at his wearing a coat in this weather. Eyes of deepest blue contemplated something far off, gradually swiveling around and focusing on Rex. For all Rex knew, this character was not entirely right in the head, or a can short of a six-pack, as Campbell would say.

"Morning," he said to the man, who had been digging a rectangular hole, only slightly larger than the iron casket that stood beside it on the sparse grass. A mound of sandy topsoil sat on the opposite side of the open gravelet, which evinced a pungent smell of earth and decomposing leaves. "I keep running into your cat."

"Macavity," the transient said.

" 'You may meet him in a by-street,' " Rex quoted, " 'You may see him in the square/But when a crime's discovered, then Macavity's not there!' I remember that poem from school." It was one of the few, along with the poem by Coleridge about the albatross and Wordsworth's rhyming verse describing a host of golden daffodils.

" 'Macavity, the Mystery Cat,' by T. S. Eliot," the man in the blue coat acknowledged. "Macavity is the name I bestowed on him many years ago when we befriended each other."

The man, whose appearance and gruff voice were at acute odds with his diction, spoke through a hole in his russet beard and in so doing, displayed the brown roots of teeth missing all along the bottom row. Rex, remembering the packet of Life Savers in his pocket, offered him one. As he approached with the packet, he caught a mild whiff of mildew and unwashed flesh. The homeless man dug out an orange candy with a dirty fingernail, prompting Rex to suggest he take the whole packet.

"Most kind. I'm Willie."

Rex introduced himself in turn. As Willie lifted the candy to his mouth, Rex noticed one of a pair of fake brass buttons missing from the cuff of his blue coat, a spiral of matching thread dangling in its absence. His heartbeat quickened.

"Are you from foreign parts?" the man inquired. "I note an accent."

"Scotland. I'm staying at the Dolphin Inn."

A look of wariness crept into the vagrant's face,

weathered by the elements and mapped with spider veins about the coarse nose, which almost looked as though it had been eaten by wormwood. "The Dolphin Inn is an old haunt of mine," he divulged in his deliberate manner. "Until the owners caught me shopping through the trash and chased me off with threats of poisoning the contents."

"The late or younger owners?" Rex asked.

"The dried up old hag and her stingy husband. All the same, I did not wish them ill. 'Misfortune has not made a coffin of my heart,' to quote Mr. Brownlow in *Oliver Twist*. I have a warm, dry place to sleep, and sleep I do, totally at peace among the dead. I tend the flowers left by mourners, and the guardian of these Elysian Fields tolerates my nocturnal presence in exchange for work."

Willie dislodged another candy from the multicolored tube. The tip of his tongue poked through the hole before retracting it into his toothless mouth. He proceeded to savor it as Macavity must have done his tuna.

"Keep Macavity away from the Dolphin Inn, if you can," Rex warned. "A cat was found poisoned there. I sought you out, Willie, because I thought you might have seen some strange goings-on three nights ago in the vicinity of the bed-and-breakfast."

"Strange things going on indeed. Why would you think I saw anything?"

"I found your coat button on Sunday morning, across the street from the alley."

Willie glanced down the front of his coat and found all the buttons accounted for.

"From your right sleeve," Rex said, pointing.

"Any chance of further victuals?"

"What is your preference?"

"Pizza, soft crust, with anchovies on the side for my cat. Macavity is partial to anchovies."

"Consider it done. What can you tell me?"

"All in good time, my friend. Return this evening after seven. I'll make sure the gate on Frances is unlocked. May I first ask about your interest in the Dyers' demise?" Willie asked.

"How did you know about their deaths?"

Willie regarded him through quizzical blue eyes. "I read the papers same as anybody else. Plenty left lying around. In any case, you referred to them as the 'late' Dyers. Were you a friend of theirs?"

"I never met them, but my hobby is solving murder cases, and I happened to be in Key West the morning the bodies were found."

"Fortuitous, indeed." Willie scratched his bushy red beard as he continued to study Rex with unnerving blue eyes. "I did see something, but I don't want to be questioned by the police. I wish only to be left alone."

"I understand, but you don't want to be responsible for that person or persons killing again, do you?"

"Years ago I relinquished all responsibility. Time was I had a house, a family, a college teaching post. I was a modern authority on Dickens. But all became meaningless and counterfeit. I took solace in the bottle and roamed our fine land. It's hard to stick out like a sore thumb in this carnival place, this phantasmagoria of life. The downest and outest feel right at home in this city."

Rex removed his pipe and a plaid cloth pouch of Clan tobacco from his pants pocket. "What did you see, Willie, the night the innkeepers were murdered? Don't worry, I'll be back this evening with the pizza." Whether Willie provided the information or not, he would never dream of denying the poor soul a meal.

"I saw the murderer. Not clear as day, but enough to ascertain certain details."

Rex methodically filled the bowl of his pipe as he listened with growing anticipation. This could be the pivotal moment where a flash of clarity beamed through the fog. However, patience was crucial. He did not want to scare Willie.

The homeless man began to speak. "He held a knife to Mrs. Dyer's neck and forced her husband to unlock the door. It was dark, the only light being toward the back of the alley, and then briefly when the door opened."

"Can you give me a description?"

"I caught a glimpse of what they were wearing. The Dyers were in clown costumes. The man had a black beard."

"A fake beard?"

Willie considered for a moment, staring hard at his shovel. "I couldn't tell."

"Might he have been dressed as a pirate?"

"Could be."

"Any other physical details you recall?"

"He was of larger build than either of the Dyers."

Which was not saying much, since they had appeared quite short, seen slumped in the kitchen. "What sort of knife was he holding?" Rex asked.

"A long, glinting one, like a fillet knife."

"Did you see a woman?"

"Eh?"

"Was there a woman besides Mrs. Dyer?"

"Only the old witch. I thought at the time it was a burglary in progress. It never occurred to my befuddled brain that they might be murdered, as indicated in the papers. I remember thinking it would serve them right if the family silver got stolen."

"What time was this?"

"Late. One or two in the morning. I don't wear a watch."

Any of the guests or family could have murdered the elder Dyers in their bed, and yet the couple had been forced through the dark alley at knifepoint.

"Thanks, Willie. I'll return later with the pizza and anchovies." Rex paused as he turned to leave. "By the way, what is in that casket you're burying? Personal possessions?"

The homeless man cast a stricken look at the iron box on the ground. "I'm preparing Macavity's burial plot. It's hard work digging into this rock, I can tell you. He's been ailing lately, though he seems to have gotten a new lease on life suddenly."

Rex reflected that it could not be much of an extended lease, judging by the state of the poor arthritic creature. Macavity looked as though he had lived every one of his nine lives, and then some. Though not ginger like his namesake in the T. S. Eliot poem, he appeared to have the same wily and elusive characteristics, but even these could not save him from inevitable old age.

"Well, for goodness' sake, keep him away from the Dolphin Inn," Rex reiterated. "Someone's been putting oleander in the compost and perhaps adding bait."

Taking his leave of Willie, he took a detour through another part of the cemetery, passing the Jewish section where small stones had been left for the dead instead of flowers, and becoming absorbed in the gravestone inscriptions along the way. Some of them were quite amusing: "I TOLD YOU I WAS SICK." Another inscription read:

160

"KERMIT FORBES — ONE HELL OF A
MAN
TEC 4  US ARMY
WORLD WAR II
JAN 6 1914   FEB 16 2000
LOVINGLY KNOWN AS SHINE
SPARRED WITH HEMINGWAY"

A small American flag stood by limply in salute.
A vase of flowers beside it had toppled over, and
Rex set it back upright. He rejoined a main path
just as a midsize commercial jet flew overhead
toward the airport at the far end of the island,
interrupting the peace and serenity. A white statue
of an angel holding a wreath lent grace to the
surrounding tombs embedded in the sandy grass
and engraved with often-recurring English and
Spanish names. Helen would be pleased he had
done a spot of sightseeing this morning, he
reflected. The cemetery was certainly well worth a
visit.

On the way back to the B & B, he digested the
nugget of information Willie had given him,
pondering the identity of the man with the black
beard. Or was finding the button off Willie's coat
and the transient's witness account of the murders
too much of a coincidence? And yet, it was all Rex
had for now, and he decided to treat it at face
value.

Dennis Barber had a fake black beard, and most probably Chuck Shumaker had worn one as part as his Captain Morgan disguise. Ryan could have procured one easily enough, as well. Although the student had been dressed as a vampire, he could have changed into a different costume the night of the murder. Pirates prevailed at Fantasy Fest. There was, unfortunately, an embarrassment of black beards—assuming the vagrant's memory could be relied upon, impaired as it might be by drink.

Willie would have known about the clown costumes from the newspaper stories. From there, a black beard was not a great stretch of the imagination. He may have been saying what Rex wanted to hear in the hope of a hot meal, or to throw him off the scent. Nonetheless, in spite of the Victorian melodrama and vaudeville connotations conjured up by such an obvious theatrical device, it was a lead Rex felt he must pursue to its resolution or dead end.

## ~EIGHTEEN~

As Rex walked back to the Dolphin Inn, he enumerated the main components of the case in his head: An obsessive-compulsive son who collected moths in his spare time and had wanted to run the Dolphin Inn; a divorced daughter in the process of vicariously murdering her ex; a succession of stray cats left dead on the doorstep; and a homeless man who claimed to have seen the murderer force the Dyers into their kitchen—a murderer with a black beard.

So absorbed was Rex that he arrived at the bed-and-breakfast before he knew it. A note Helen had left in their suite informed him she had gone on a shopping spree with Rosa Diaz. Probably the two women would lunch together in town. Just as he was plotting his next course of action, a light tap sounded at the door, and Rex opened it.

Walt stood on the other side next to a crate on

wheels piled high with clean towels and folded sheets. "Would you like me to do up your room?" he asked.

"Come in," Rex said, stepping aside. "Are you still managing okay on your own?"

"Oh, you know how it is," Walt hemmed, entering the en-suite bathroom with fresh towels.

"No need to do the bed," Rex said when he returned with an armful of used towels. "Helen is fastidious about making it up in the morning."

"So I see. A woman after my own heart." Walt looked around the room to see what else needed to be done. He inspected the vase of fresh flowers on the dresser and emptied the wastepaper basket into a transparent plastic bag.

"Did you dress up for Fantasy Fest?" Rex asked conversationally as Walt loaded the bag on the cart.

"Heavens, no." The innkeeper hitched the thick glasses up the bridge of his nose and rested a hand on a flaccid hip in a pose Rex supposed was meant to be casual. "I don't like disguises myself. Merle and Taffy enjoyed it, but I always think it's rather silly when adults dress up."

"Which is pretty much what everyone does in Key West at the end of October, it seems."

"This island attracts free spirits and fun-lovers." Walt obviously did not count among them. "Why do you ask?"

"I heard from a potential witness that your

parents were seen with a black-bearded man shortly before they were murdered."

"Goodness! But that could be anyone. Chuck Shumaker and Dennis Barber were both wearing black beards that night. Not to mention countless other revelers."

Rex did not yet see what motive either guest could have had. Nor were they at the B and B long enough to have poisoned the cats—if indeed the Dyers' murderer was responsible for that too. He decided to take a chance and catch Walt off his guard. Before he could, Walt asked tentatively, "So, you're investigating my parents' murders. I heard something about that."

"Nerium oleander, Walt. Traces were found in your compost." He watched Walt's bespectacled face carefully. The doughy features seemed to dissolve before his eyes. "A reasonable explanation for the poison being in there might help clarify things," Rex prompted.

"I have oleander growing all over the yard, as you probably know. It grows fast and needs regular trimming to keep under control." Sweat beaded Walt's temples. This was not the version he had given police. Captain Diaz had reported that Walt had denied all knowledge of the plant being in the trash can.

"Walt." Rex assumed a kind but authoritative tone, to which the timid man would hopefully respond and cave. "The amount found in the compost did not constitute serious pruning. And it was crushed up. It was obviously there for a purpose."

"Okay!" Walt squeaked. "I just wanted my parents to take early retirement before they ran the Dolphin into the ground. Their nest egg, they called it, ha! I would've told prospective buyers about the dead cats to scare them off too, and told them the place was haunted. Whatever it took! When they were in Vermont this summer, it was running perfect with just Raf and me. But they had to interfere." The innkeeper bowed his head. "I poisoned some fish and left it in the trash can with the lid half off and then put the cats on the doorstep before the guests woke up. After Taffy saw them, I got rid of them. She was so delusional, she didn't realize everybody hated her. She was always putting on airs, talking about how much she was leaving to her heirs and flaunting her rings!"

Walt sank onto the reproduction Victorian chair. "My prayers came true!" He opened his hands in wonderment. "But I never actually wanted my parents dead. I never dreamed they'd be murdered and I'd be running the place." He looked as stunned as a newly minted lottery winner. He then rose from the chair and, wheeling the crate after him, took off down the landing, muttering that he was truly sorry about the cats.

Either Walt was innocent or else he was one of

the best actors Rex had ever come across. In any case, he deplored Walt's poisoning of the alley cats.

He needed a puff of his pipe and went out onto the balcony to light it. The peaty-vanilla aroma of Clan tobacco wafted into the air around him as he rocked in his chair and surveyed the kidney-shaped pool, the sun reflecting off the undisturbed surface. The plastic slatted lounge chair that Diane had occupied the previous day stood vacant in the same place, along with the magazine and metal ashtray. He settled more comfortably into the blue cushions and pensively puffed away at his pipe, his gaze through the white railings resting upon the thriving bougainvillea and pink oleander masking the property-line fence.

He deliberated contacting Captain Diaz and imparting the information he had managed to elicit from Walt and Willie. He could grab a bite to eat on the way. With these plans in mind, he headed back down the stairs, but when he reached the front door, he paused. Was Willie a credible witness? He was educated, but did he have all his marbles? He probably drank more than he should and, while he had not appeared drunk at the cemetery, his memory, by his own admission, might not function as it used to. Perhaps further thought and corroboration were required on the subject of the alleged assailant with the black beard. Plus, he did not truly relish the idea of having lunch by himself.

"Are you going out?" Diane asked, coming up the hall from the guest lounge.

"I am unable to decide," he replied with a sheepish smile. "I got stood up for lunch."

"I was just about to fix myself a sandwich. Would you like one?"

"That would be grand—if you don't mind. I know this is not a bed-and-lunch place."

"Oh, please. And anyway, I wanted to pick your brains about something."

"Of course," he said. "Perhaps I can pick yours in return."

"Deal. Egg salad sandwich okay?"

"Perfect."

"I'll bring it through to the dining room. We won't be disturbed. Walt went to Pritchard's to finalize the funeral arrangements."

Rex sat down at one of the tables cleared of breakfast items. He wondered what Diane wanted to ask him. He did not have long to wait. From a tray she produced two plates, two glasses, and a pitcher of cold tea filled with ice and lemon slices. Also, a small legal pad and a pencil.

Rex took a bite of the egg mayonnaise on lettuce sandwich and complimented her. The tea she poured out for them was good, too, if a little sweet. But who was he to look a gift horse in the mouth? Lunch had been provided, and he now had an opportunity to question Diane further.

"You first," he said.

"Okay. So, what, in your opinion, is the best way to go about killing someone?"

Rex almost choked on his bread. "We are talking hypothetically?" he sought to confirm.

Diane studied him, the skin around her green eyes crinkling in amusement. "What do you think?"

"Okay... Well, I'll need some specifics. For starters, what age is the victim? Male? Female? Weight, *et cetera?*"

"Male, six-one, two hundred pounds. Forty-one years old."

"That's specific, certainly. Is this a character in your novel?"

"Uh-huh." Diane bit into her sandwich and chewed thoughtfully for a minute. "It's also my ex."

"And you want to kill him off in your book?"

"Passionately. Along with his skanky girlfriend."

"How much do you want to make him suffer?"

"Enough to make him sorry."

"I'm sure you could get imaginative ideas on how to do away with your character in any number of novels."

"That's fiction. And usually in true crime books the perpetrator has been caught, so the murder had a flaw. My heroine must get away with it."

169

"The simplest ideas usually work best in real life," Rex suggested from his experience as a prosecutor. Diane prepared to make notes in her pad. "The means of death," he continued, "is probably less important than the execution. Problem is, in the case of a murdered ex, the first person the police look at is the partner, unless the victim was killed during a bank hold-up or in a car accident, or some such random circumstance. Otherwise the spouse has to have a watertight alibi."

"That's why a lot of spouses resort to contract killers." Diane speculatively tapped her pencil against her teeth. "But my heroine wouldn't derive the same satisfaction from that. She'd much prefer to see him squirm firsthand."

"Well, I hope I've given you something to think aboot," Rex said with certain misgivings. "I hope it becomes a bestseller, and then you can name one of the suites at the Dolphin Inn after yourself!" *If you don't go to prison first.* "And be careful of libel," he cautioned, the lawyerly side of him coming to the fore. "If your ex recognizes himself in your book and doesn't like what he reads, he could sue."

"I'll disguise him so no one will know it's him."

Rex regarded Diane with curiosity. Was she over her ex? She certainly held a grudge. "I hope you have better luck with a man next time," he said.

Diane gave a snort of derision. "Fat chance. I'm saddled with two kids. When do I get the chance to go out?"

"Working at a bed-and-breakfast must give you an opportunity to meet people."

She gave this some thought. "It's mainly couples staying here. Quite a few Germans, some Brits. You're the sort of guy I'd like to meet if you were single. Steady and dependable. Helen is very lucky to have you. And she knows it."

"I hope so, and thank you."

"You said you had something I might be able to help you with?" Diane resumed munching on her sandwich while Rex refilled their iced tea.

It was another long shot. "Black-beard," he said.

"Black beard or Blackbeard, as in the pirate, Edward Teach?"

"Either."

"Hm." Diane wiped a crumb from the corner of her mouth with a folded napkin off the table. "Are you referring to Taffy's little joke?"

"What joke would that be?"

"It's dumb. She told me she had a fancy man on the side. This was after I found her with an expensive bottle of gin, the blue one with the portrait of Queen Victoria on the label. My father would never have gotten Bombay Sapphire for her, and she couldn't have bought it herself since he held the purse strings. He made a note of every

171

purchase in a ledger. But she was getting it from somewhere and hiding it from him. Taffy was very cunning."

Apparently so, Rex thought, remembering the stash found in the nooks and crannies of the Dyers' private suite.

"I know I shouldn't talk about her like that, but she made our lives miserable, Walt's and mine. At least I got away for a while."

Out of the frying pan into the fire, Rex thought, reflecting on how Diane's marriage must have been, toward the end anyway. He pushed his empty plate away and leaned in toward her, elbows on the table, receptive to hearing what else she had to say.

"She said this Blackbeard guy bought her the booze. He was probably named for Captain Morgan. Though I don't know why she didn't call him Gordon or Stoli after her favorite tipples. Rum gave her migraines. But then again, she wasn't the most rational person on the planet. She acquired a new clown figurine from somewhere, which broke in a fight with Chuck Shumaker." Diane shook her head slowly. "I know for a fact my father didn't buy that horror for her. They didn't have any spare cash. Either she drank it all or she was in rehab, which was even more expensive."

"If Lover Boy didn't exist, how did she get hold of the items herself?"

"Good question. I gave up asking because she always gave me the same answer, along with her knowing little smirk. She could have shoplifted the stuff, for all I know."

Rex sat back in his chair, headachy from the refrain of black beards that kept playing like a catchy and annoying tune in his brain.

When shortly afterward he went upstairs, he found Helen back from her shopping date with Rosa. She kicked off her sandals, complaining of tired feet from all the walking. The hum of a vacuum cleaner started up on the landing, forming a tightening in front of his strained eyes.

"We had fun," Helen told him. "I'm no longer miffed about not going to Mexico. I'm having a fabulous time, and I hope you are, too, in your own peculiar way." She stepped up on her tiptoes and kissed him.

"It's a very peculiar case." He told her about the recurring theme of black beards that day, first from Willie and then from Diane, leaving out the more sinister details. If Taffy did know someone by that name, who was it? he kept asking himself. And was it the person Willie saw hustling the Dyers into their guest house on Saturday night at knifepoint?

"Chuck Shumaker was dressed up as Captain Morgan for the parade, and Dennis Barber wears a fake black beard for his book signings," he pointed out to Helen.

"Barber. That's interesting, you know."

"What is?" Rex rummaged in his wash bag for aspirin.

"The word barber—as in beard. Do you think the name is a coincidence?"

Rex had to admit it had never occurred to him. Sometimes Helen came up with a gem.

## ~NINETEEN~

That afternoon at happy hour in the guest lounge, Rex suggested to the Barbers that the four of them take the wine out to the patio. He could not abide to stare at the clumsily executed paintings of tigers stalking in the tall grass, which he had learned from Diane were painted by Taffy in the days when she harbored illusions about becoming an exhibiting artist. Rex wondered why Walt didn't take them down off the walls, but then he might have substituted them with his moth collections—a dubious improvement.

The guests migrated to the tiki bar, a massive umbrella of thatched fronds with a wooden counter beneath, and four stools. Peggy wore a pair of white Capris, a modern version of her pirate pants. Helen modeled the black cotton dress she had purchased the day before, but on her curves it no longer looked simply like a long

T-shirt. Changing into it in their room, she had said it felt "cool and comfy." Rex had added something else, especially with her tanned legs and new gold sandals.

Walt brought out a couple of Citronella Candles to ward off mosquitoes. After the fraught past few days, the Dolphin Inn was beginning to settle into a more relaxed atmosphere, although Walt had requested that his remaining guests keep the front door locked at all times to avoid thrill-seekers and reporters from wandering in at will.

"Don't know if these candles actually work," Peggy said when he had left. "But they certainly smell nice and lemony."

"We'll find out soon enough," said Rex who was highly susceptible to mosquito bites. He offered the Barbers some wine.

"We're having pineapple juice," Peggy said, covering her glass with one hand.

"You don't mind if we do?" Rex nodded at the bottle he held over Helen's glass.

"Heavens, no."

He poured a glass for his fiancée and then for himself. "Walt mentioned you stayed here two years ago...," he began.

"Well, we did," Peggy said in so natural a manner that her earlier omission of the fact now seemed perfectly innocent. "Taffy and Merle were away that time, so we, uh, never had the pleasure," she trailed off diplomatically. "Walt said his mother was at a clinic and we assumed she was sick. It's obvious now she must have been drying out someplace. Walt did a great job running the guest house with that young man— what was his name again?" she asked her husband.

Dennis thought for a moment and shrugged.

"We asked after him this time around," Diane said. "But he had just left."

"Raphael," Rex supplied. "According to Walt, he was let go."

"That's it. Raf." Peggy took his measure with quick, green eyes. "My, but you have been doing your homework."

*As you've been doing yours,* Rex thought, recalling how Peggy had Googled his name and found out about his private murder investigations. She had presumably told Diane about it, which was why Walt's sister had asked him about committing the perfect murder. He still felt a little uneasy about that in light of the double homicide that had occurred under this roof.

"He was an obliging young man and very eager to improve his English," Peggy continued. "We liked him a lot, didn't we, Den?"

Dennis nodded in the affirmative. Rex asked if anything untoward had happened during that stay, and the Barbers said no, not that they remembered.

"Anyway, we enjoyed the Dolphin Inn enough

to book again this year," Peggy said with a rueful shrug. "And Walt was kind enough to give us a special rate. Last year, we stayed home in Wichita on account of our son getting married."

"How did the wedding turn out?" Helen asked to Rex's chagrin. He wanted to stay on topic.

"Oh, it was beautiful, with a theme of fall colors," Peggy replied.

"How lovely," Helen said. "We have gorgeous autumns in England too, the leaves turning russet and gold. But we're thinking about a spring wedding."

Here we go, thought Rex. He offered to refill her wine, but she made a face. It wasn't very good chardonnay. Rex topped up his glass and added ice cubes from a bowl on the bar top.

"Spring is coming up pretty fast," Peggy warned. "There's a lot to arrange for a wedding."

"Not ours," Rex interjected. "It's going to be simple."

"They always start out that way," Dennis remarked darkly.

"Is it your first wedding, Helen?" his wife inquired.

"Yes, and Rex's second."

The Barbers wished them the best and said they just knew they would be very happy together. The women hugged. Dennis reached over and shook Rex's hand in a rare show of warm fuzziness.

"We should go somewhere for dinner to celebrate," he suggested. "There's a rib joint that's not expensive, an olde-worlde sort of pub within walking distance. What do you say?"

"Lead on, my good man," Rex said with jovial humor. The word "pub" generally got his attention, and ribs sounded spot on, too.

As they rose from their stools, Helen chatted to Peggy about how she had almost finished the Barbers' book, and found it riveting. Peggy glowed with pleasure in the candlelight. She and Helen walked ahead, while he and Dennis followed, discussing American beers. It promised to be fine evening, with no threat of showers, as they made their way to the restaurant among the throngs of tourists.

Half an hour later, they were comfortably and convivially installed in their booth gnawing on Charlie's World Famous Baby Back Ribs, when Peggy suddenly blurted, "I know that man," her recollection apparently stirred by someone she saw passing in the crowd outside the window.

The person, whom Rex strained, but failed, to see could have been the visitor to the bed-and-breakfast two years ago, Peggy proceeded to explain. Rex pricked up his ears. She might not have noticed him tonight at all had Rex not asked about their previous stay at the Dolphin Inn, which sort of put her on alert, she said.

"It's as if I sensed rather than saw him just

now. I only saw the back of his head. Do you ever get that feeling?" she asked the other people at table.

"A visitor, you said?" Rex queried. "Not a guest?"

Peggy could not be sure, jokingly blaming the "onset of senility." But this man, she had thought at the time and whom she described as "a swarthy devil," was perfect for her pirate hero in *The British Brigand,* were he to be featured in a movie. Beyond that, she could not recall any further physical details. He had come to the Dolphin Inn looking for Taffy and had left dissatisfied with Walt's explanation that his mother was "recuperating" somewhere in preparation for the busy season. If Peggy had to guess, she would have said he was a bill collector. Rex asked if there had been words.

Peggy shook her head slowly, remembering. "No altercation between the two men as such, just an air of unpleasantness—and perhaps a veiled threat? But perhaps I'm imagining that, in retrospect. Dennis is always saying what a fertile imagination I have!"

Her husband dutifully agreed, and Helen smiled into her tankard of root beer. Dennis was the perfect foil to Peggy's more extrovert nature.

Had Taffy been the main target all along? Rex wondered. Peggy had not mentioned Merle in her account. As far as the murders went, the husband could have been a bonus, a precaution, or else collateral damage.

Having exhausted the topic of the Barbers' first stay at the guest house, the conversation reverted, at Peggy's prompting, to Rex and Helen's wedding and their respective families. Rex talked about his son and about his aged mother, who lived in a grand old terrace house in Edinburgh with an equally aged housekeeper, whom he had called Miss Bird since boyhood. She made phenomenal sponge cake and scones, but her eyesight, sadly, was failing, and she had been known to put salt instead of sugar into her baking. Helen, in turn, explained that her own mother had died of a stroke five years ago. Her father had remarried and emigrated to Australia, but he was going to make the trip home to walk his daughter down the aisle. She laughed a little.

"I don't think he ever thought he'd see the day. My two sisters got married eons ago."

"They say later marriages have a better rate of success," Peggy told her, squeezing her hand in encouragement.

"We can't decide to have the wedding in England or Scotland. Rex has his elderly mother to consider. She's as fit as a fiddle, but doesn't like to travel. And he has colleagues he'd like to invite. I have the staff and some kids at my school. Still, I like the idea of a Scottish wedding, with a tartan theme."

"You're leaving it a bit late," Dennis said, echoing his wife's earlier words and shaking his head in disapproval. "Spring is right around the corner."

"We plan on diving right in when we get back from holiday," Rex said. "We thought we'd take a break first."

"You'll need a break after," Dennis predicted gloomily. "Our son's wedding was a logistical nightmare. Who to invite, where to put them up. Flowers, food, photographers. It never ends."

Rex and Helen had attended a nightmare wedding in Derbyshire that didn't bear thinking about, but for different reasons. It had almost given Rex cold feet.

"Den, stop putting a damper on everything," Peggy chided. "Don't pay attention to him," she told Helen and Rex, who, for his part, was not paying him much attention at all. His mind was on other matters.

After dinner, they parted company as the Barbers wanted to return to the guest house, being early-to-bed and early-to-rise folk. Rex and Helen preferred to stay out a while longer.

At the cupola that marked the Southernmost Point of Key West, Helen asked someone to take their picture while she and Rex posed, arms around each other. Afterward, they strolled the length of Duval. It was not quite dusk yet, but the air had cooled, and it felt good to be out and about among the cheerful crowds. A man and his German Shepherd begged on the sidewalk. The dog, dressed in a Captain Morgan hat, sunglasses, and Mardi Gras beads, lay nonchalantly, forepaws extended, as tourists took photos and filled the bucket with dollar bills.

The tourist couple gazed in leisurely fashion at the elegant guest houses and into windows displaying souvenirs, swimsuits, and T-shirts. They passed ice cream parlors, a homemade cookie and fudge shop wafting tantalizing aromas onto the street, and smoothie stands stocked with exotic fruit. They listened outside bars to live music, and peered into hand-blown glass and picture galleries.

"Are we looking for anything in particular?" Helen asked after a while. The sun had disappeared behind the façades of the buildings in a vermilion ball of fire, and she pulled her cardigan out of her shoulder bag.

"Just thought it would be nice to walk off those ribs and garlic mashed potato."

"And fried onion rings," Helen added. "And banana split."

"I confess to a weakness for American food. Except grits." The Americans could keep their grits, though he had to concede they probably felt the same way about kippers and kidneys for breakfast.

"It's so unlike you to wander about aimlessly,

and I spent the better part of today walking around the shops with Rosa."

Not like Helen to complain either, but she was right. "Fair enough," he said. "Well, to be perfectly frank, I'm on the look-out for a certain establishment."

"What sort of establishment?"

"I'm not altogether sure, but a biker at the police station referred to it as the House of the Rising Sun, and mentioned girls. I assumed it would be on Duval."

"It's probably a knocking shop," Helen said. "Perhaps that's why there's no big sign over the door. I've been up and down Duval a dozen times and I don't remember seeing anything by that name."

"The girls could be waitresses working at a folk-rock bar."

"Rex, I know you had a strict Presbyterian upbringing, but sometimes you can be so naïve."

"It's just that I can't see Walt being associated with a place such as you describe."

"Walt?" Helen expressed surprise. "Well, you never know. Though I'd have thought he's more likely to be looking at naughty pictures."

"I know what you mean." The notion of Walt being a closet pervert had not escaped Rex, whatever Helen said about his upbringing. No question, the innkeeper was a strange individual.

They continued to scrutinize the bistros and

restaurants. At the storefront of a costume and lingerie store, white clown masks with round red noses, rubbery lips, and stringy orange hair sticking out at the sides seemed to jeer at Rex for not having solved the Dyer case.

"Sod off," he told the grinning masks topping the star-spangled clown suits.

"Are you talking to those clowns?" Helen asked in amusement. "They look harmless enough to me."

Not to Rex. He found he was developing an aversion to clowns. "If it is, as you say, a house of ill repute, and it's on Duval, it's more likely to be at the quieter end of the street," he decided.

Trudging back in that direction, he entered a convenience store and made inquiries. To his embarrassment, the House of the Rising Sun, far from being a bar, proved to be what Helen had supposed, and the store clerk gave him complicit and explicit directions as to its whereabouts.

"You're blushing to your red roots," Helen noted when he re-emerged onto the sidewalk.

"I wish you had come in with me. I think I was mistaken for a john."

Helen laughed outright, but had the grace not to say, "I told you so." He led her across the busy street and down one block to a private residence with an innocuous façade lit with fairy lights. "This must be it. Looks respectable enough..."

"Are you proposing to go inside?" Helen

inquired with a distinct lift of her left eyebrow.

"I don't think that will be necessary. I was just curious."

"Curiosity got the cat," she quipped.

"And satisfaction got him back—and made him fat."

Why did everything keep coming back to cats? And black beards? He was reminded of an errand.

"Ready to head back?" Helen asked.

"Not quite," he prevaricated.

"Oh, and what other entertainment have you got planned for us this evening?" she asked with an ironic smile.

"I promised I would deliver a pizza to the cemetery."

Her expression changed to one of total stupefaction, tinged with dismay. "I see. Well, never let it be said you don't know how to show a girl a good time," she muttered, and added: "How far?"

# ~TWENTY~

"Watch your step," Rex cautioned as they stumbled between toppling gravestones and vine-choked tombs silhouetted beneath a pale moon intermittently obscured by whispering palm fronds. Barely sufficient light enabled him to find his way without tripping over and dropping the flat cardboard box, from which escaped the fishy aroma of anchovies. All the same, he wished he'd thought to bring a small flashlight. The cemetery looked nothing like it did during the day.

"What is Willie like?" Helen inquired.

"Willie is somewhat poetic. He talks in quotes. I think he used to teach English." The man had clearly fallen on hard times. Wasn't that a novel by Dickens?

"And this is where he lives?" Helen asked incredulously.

"He has a makeshift shelter here. He said the

caretaker lets him stay in return for doing odd jobs around the place. Willie is quite a character. I think you'll appreciate him."

"I'm sure I will. Goodness, I'm glad I wore sandals and not heels. I never expected to be hiking up and down Duval Street all evening and trekking across a pitch-black graveyard."

"This way." Rex led her off at a tangent, recalling landmarks from his previous visit, a broken urn here, a tall cross there, a peculiar configuration of headstones.

After a few minutes, he glimpsed an orange pinprick of light bobbing in the dark, and made his way toward it, Helen close behind him. He found Willie seated on his raised slab smoking the glowing butt of a cigarette. A bed of leaves overlaid by a canvas sheet covered the ground beneath the tombstone, reinforced on three sides by cardboard and corrugated iron to shield him from the elements.

"Welcome to my boudoir," Willie said.

"Where is Macavity?" was the first question out of Rex's mouth as he looked around for the vagrant's faithful old cat.

"Rest easy, my friend. He is still with us in the land of the living. But he is a nocturnal creature, and his instinct is to hunt." Willie spoke in his slow gruff voice, carefully enunciating his words around missing teeth. "On occasion he is still able to catch some prey, and brings it back as an offering to the gods."

"I think it's just a gift for you," Helen said sensibly, staying close to Rex. "I had a cat that left birds and mice on my back doorstep."

"My fiancée Helen," Rex introduced her.

Willie stood up but hesitated to take her hand. He seemed shy in her presence and averted his eyes. He took the pizza box with mumbled thanks and set it down on the stone slab.

"Do you have everything you need here?" Helen asked with tender-hearted concern.

"A dry place to sleep, a drop of wine to warm my heart and my thoughts, and I am content."

"Rex said you were an English teacher?"

"An adjunct professor of literature at a revered college. I told my students to stop wasting their time reading longwinded critiques by academics who couldn't write a novel to save their lives, and to go—go!—out into the world and see and write about it themselves. A long story. And in short, I was fired." His toothless mouth clamped shut and disappeared into his beard.

Rex thought sadly that Willie's drinking might have had something to do with his professional decline.

"I am reduced to frequenting the library and opening books I cannot keep. I love the smell of new books. I would go into Borders Express and fill my lungs with the rarefied scent of virgin paper." Willie held his nose aloft and closed his eyes as if to conjure up the scent and savor it—a feat indeed over the reek of anchovy and pepperoni. "But, sadly, it closed."

Rex felt Helen's elbow nudge him gently. "Well, let us not detain you further," he said, finding himself elevating his diction in the vagrant's presence. "Unless there's anything you've remembered since our conversation this morning?"

"The scene at the Dolphin Inn is as I described it. The dark beard, the glinting knife or dagger, the clown costumes, the Dyers cowed and cooperative."

"Thank you, Willie." Rex was encouraged that the homeless man had recalled their conversation down to the last detail. He had even added a couple of embellishments, namely the dagger and the attitude of the Dyers in the face of their ordeal, both of which seemed plausible under the circumstances. It proved Willie could retain information over limited periods of time at least. "Enjoy your meal," he said.

"I shall. I thank you."

As Rex and Helen moved away, a white bib and forepaws appeared in the dark from behind a gravestone, where Macavity must have been waiting. Leaping onto the tomb, he began pawing the box that Willie had set on his lap.

"Patience, my good fellow," Willie bid him. "The anchovies are all for you."

"How sad," Helen said when they were out of earshot.

"You never cried over the Dyers," Rex pointed out, guiding her by the hand.

"I never met them."

"Probably wouldn't have made a difference if you had." He was beginning to think there was no one at all to mourn the old couple, not even their children.

At night the presence of the tens of thousands of interred and entombed bodies felt almost palpable. Headstones stuck out of the ground in a semi-circle of crooked teeth, the gnarled arms of trees reaching out fingers to snag their hair as they passed. Breaths of a breeze licked Rex's neck. Or perhaps it was instinct alerting him to some unseen danger and making his hairs stand on end. A twig cracked in the darkness as an owl let out a loud *to-wit, to-woo*. Startled, Helen tripped on a piece of masonry lodged in the ground, and Rex hastened to steady her.

A milky glow rose in the clearing around them, deathly quiet but for the rustle of nocturnal creatures in the shadowed leaves and undergrowth. He had spotted several large iguanas earlier in the day, and knowing Helen's aversion to reptiles, hoped they did not come toe to toe with one, or else eye to eye with one in the trees. He was relieved when he saw the Frances Street gate in the distance. Helen had begun to limp slightly.

"How are you bearing up?" he asked.

"My sandals are beginning to rub, but it's only a few blocks to the B and B. I can take them off when we reach the street."

Rex was extremely apologetic when she showed him the red blisters on her toes under a streetlamp, but she said it had been in a good cause.

Partly in a good cause, he reflected, but whether their night excursions led to a break in the case was less certain. At this point it boiled down to a killer with a black beard, if Willie was to be believed. Yet this did fit Peggy Barber's description of a "swarthy" visitor who had come to the Dolphin Inn looking for Taffy two years ago. Furthermore, Diane had said her mother's supplier of gin and baubles was someone called Blackbeard.

Good luck finding this character, he told himself.

By the time he and Helen reached the Dolphin Inn, they were more than ready for their comfortable four-poster bed. Rex glanced at his watch: almost eleven. The front door was locked. Helen brushed the soles of her feet on the indoor mat, and noiselessly they mounted the stairs in order not to disturb the Barbers, who had gone to bed early.

At the turn in the banister, Rex heard a door on

the above landing open and close with a thud. Michelle's and Ryan's voices whispered urgently together as their key was loudly inserted and turned in the lock. Young people were not always respectful of other peoples' repose, Rex considered more censoriously than he might otherwise have done had he not been so bone-weary and aware of his earlier headache making a comeback. He cleared his throat and jangled his keys to announce his presence downstairs. They might have been discussing something private, and he drew the line at eavesdropping on conversations unless the speakers were raising their voices.

The young couple appeared on his floor, dressed to go out, Ryan's hair still wet or perhaps gelled, Michelle wearing a short red sequined dress. The four of them exchanged goodnights as Rex and Helen entered their room.

He opened the balcony doors to air the room, but did not sit outside taking in the night air on this particular occasion. He was too tired and, much as he was loath to admit to himself, a little discouraged with progress in the case. Where did one begin to look for a stranger with a black beard, or a person disguised with one?

The next time he stood on his balcony, early the following morning and still in his dressing gown, he had to rub his eyes to make sure he was not dreaming. A female body lay motionless at the bottom of the kidney-shaped pool.

## ~TWENTY-ONE~

Rex raced down the stairs, desperate to save the young woman if there still remained a chance. Thoughts raced through his mind. Where was Ryan? Did Michelle's guardians still live in Vermont? Walt would have to contact them with the sad news of her death. How and why had this happened? And had it to do with the Dyers' murders?

The money she had been left was the obvious conclusion. He ran through to the guest lounge where the drapes were drawn across the glass sliders. His sleep-stiffened fingers wrangled with the catch. He finally burst onto the patio.

Face down on the pool floor at the deep end, long dark hair undulating beneath the surface strewn with bougainvillea petals blown from the bushes, the clothed woman was incontestably dead. A long red scarf leashed around her neck had been suctioned into the outlet drain. Now that he was nearer the victim, he realized, with some measure of relief, that it was not in fact Michelle Cuzzens in the water. From the balcony he had confused the water-darkened hair with the girl's raven tresses. This woman was tall too, but curvier. Who was she? Not a guest at the Dolphin Inn, and yet she did seem familiar.

He speculated she had been choked by the scarf, leaving no more evidence than in the strangulation of the Dyers. Drowning the victim outright would have proved a riskier process, involving more resistance and a certain amount of splashing. Several windows overlooked the pool. Even dumping a dead body in here was chancy. So why chance it? Another statement being made, he reasoned.

Walt materialized beside him, mouth agape. "You...what...how?" he began, echoing Rex's own questions.

"Call Detective Diaz on this number." Rex thrust the business card at him which he'd had the presence of mind to snatch up from the desk in his room. "Quick!"

Walt staggered off to phone the detective, glancing in horror over his shoulder. Helen called out to Rex from their balcony. "Listen, I thought... Oh, my God! Rex! Is that... Surely not a dead body in the pool?" She clamped a hand to her mouth.

Rex entertained the fleeting and inconsequential thought that the balcony scene was somewhat farcical, save for the tragic circumstances.

"Walt went to ring the police. Stay upstairs," he told Helen. "And lock the door."

"Is she the woman we saw the other night? The one wearing a red silk scarf? I can't believe it..."

Rex kneeled as close to the edge of the pool as he dared without compromising potential evidence, and attempted to get a better look at the corpse. The jewelry on her arm and hands glittered under the sun-refracted surface.

"Poor lass," he muttered to himself.

"I never saw her before." Walt, returned from his mission to call the police, hovered at a short distance.

"Well, what is she doing in your pool?"

"I have no idea!"

"Where's Diane?"

"Not here yet."

"Who else is around?"

"No-no one," Walt stammered. "I mean, Michelle and Ryan will still be in bed. They usually get up late. They're staying for free until the funeral. Michelle is family, after all, and they don't have much money," he went on, talking for the sake of talking. "At least not until the insurance company pays up. The Barbers should be down for breakfast soon. What are they going to think?"

"Where were you last night?" Rex could not be sure when the drowning took place, but the woman was dressed up as for a night on the town. As the students had been.

Walt's nose twitched. His timid gaze reverted to the body in the pool. "I went out at ten-thirty."

"Until what time?"

"Midnight. I never checked back here. No reason to. I went straight to bed."

Ryan and Michelle had left the guest house at around eleven. Rex and Helen had gone to bed shortly thereafter. The balcony doors to their suite were open all night. He had not heard a thing, and it was unlikely Helen had either since she took sleeping pills on vacation. If the Barbers had been asleep, there would have been no lights on at the back of the bed-and-breakfast from eleven o' clock or so until Michelle and Ryan returned, possibly sometime in the wee hours of the morning. The killer/s might have seen Walt leave on his moped and waited until the coast was clear. These thoughts flooded Rex's brain in a swirling tsunami.

"The police will want to know where you went," he told Walt.

"I'd rather not say."

"Why not?"

"People would get the wrong impression."

"What sort of impression are they going to get now?" Rex pointed into the pool. "If you have an alibi, all to the good."

"Why did this have to happen last night?" the innkeeper wailed. "I hardly ever go out."

"So, where did you go?"

"Nowhere."

Rex curbed his impatience. "If by chance it has anything to do with the House of the Rising Sun, it can't be worse than having another murder at your B and B." Bed-and-breakfast-*and*-bodies, Rex thought. "In fact, it seems you have been doing some good deeds at the Rising Sun."

Walt had started guiltily at each mention of the establishment. "No good deed goes unpunished," he griped. "Not sure where you got your information." He regarded Rex with suspicion and a hint of resentment. "But okay then, I used to work there as a part-time assistant manager to subsidize what my parents were paying me. Jobs are not that easy to come by around here," he said in his defense. "My job was to oversee the girls and make sure the clients didn't try anything on, beyond what they paid for."

Rex had difficulty imagining Walt in the role of enforcer, but nodded in encouragement for him to continue.

"These are just ordinary girls trying to make ends meet," Walt explained. "Most of them can't even reconcile their checkbooks. I loaned one of them rent money so she wouldn't get evicted. I still go over once in a while to make sure they're okay. That's where I was last night." A pause. "How did you know?"

"Twisted Angel sang your praises."

At first Walt looked dumbstruck, and then beamed under his thick glasses. "Angel—he's like a legend around the island. And a good guy to have on your side."

Rex reflected that he, personally, would not want to get on the biker's bad side.

"But this whole thing is a disaster," Walt mumbled, gazing back into the pool, and then looking away quickly. "Things were just beginning to get back to normal."

When was it ever normal? Rex wondered.

"Swimming in stilettos?" Detective Diaz asked behind them, making Rex jump. "I'd recognize those ankles anywhere. Keep back, now. We're gonna have to process the area." He got on his cell phone and issued brief instructions to the person at the other end as he visually scanned the surroundings. "Chances slim to none we can lift footprints off this aggregate concrete pool deck," he said, mostly to himself, before cutting the connection.

Walt besieged him, a blubbering wreck. "Who is targeting my B and B?" he wailed.

"Wish I knew." Diaz strode over to the fence and, grabbing the pool skimmer, extended the net under the water and tilted the blurry face toward him.

"Connie Lamont?" Rex asked for the sake of confirmation.

"Looks that way." Diaz lifted her right hand, tipped in red nail polish, and examined it through the water. He straightened, extracted the dripping pole from the deep end, and turned to Walt. "Any idea what she's doing in your pool?"

"No, and Mr. Graves already asked."

"Well, now I'm asking."

I don't know, and I don't know her. Never saw her before."

Rex wondered about the woman's family, who would be duly notified. Diaz had said she was from Ft. Lauderdale on vacation.

"And did either of you see or hear anything?" Diaz, himself freshly shaved, took in Rex's navy cotton flannel dressing gown wrapped over pale blue pajamas, a gleam of amused disbelief in his eyes.

"I'm afraid not. Our room is that one up there." Rex pointed to the end balcony on the right. "The French doors were open all night, but I was out like a light, slept like a log, and was up with the birds, to use all the clichés in the book. I stepped out on the balcony this morning to gauge the weather, and that's when I spotted the body."

"And thought you were still dreaming," Diaz said, adding a cliché.

"I admit to rubbing my eyes and taking a second look. It was a shock. At first I thought it was Michelle Cuzzens because of the long hair."

"Lucky for you that you were out on the Atlantic on the first leg of your cruise when the first two murders went down, huh? And what about you, Mr. Dyer? Did you hear or see anything last night?" the detective asked routinely.

"Nothing."

"And where were you?"

"Asleep in my suite."

Rex flicked him a look. Walt had told him he went out at ten-thirty.

"It's got no windows," the innkeeper blabbed. "Except for a small frosted glass one in the bathroom high up in the wall. Could it have been an accident? I heard of a case in the lower Keys where a drunk dude's thingy got sucked into the pool filter."

"We'll find out if this lady was drinking, if she could've fell in. I'd like to know what she was doing at the Dolphin Inn."

"You and me both," Walt complained.

"Did either of you touch anything?"

"No," Rex answered. "I got close enough to see if there was any hope of resuscitation, that's all."

"You seen a drowned victim before?"

"I have, but I think cause of death in this instance might've been strangulation."

"Uh-huh." Diaz turned to Walt. "Why was the bolt not drawn on the gate to the alley? I walked right in on you guys."

"Pool man comes Wednesdays." Walt used his fingernail to scrape at an invisible speck on his shirt button.

Diaz sighed with resignation, no doubt thinking how much easier his job would be if everyone took proper safety precautions. "What time?"

"Anywhere between six and eight in the morning. He leaves a card with a check list. He's not been in yet."

"Or been in and left," Diaz said. "How long he been working here?"

"Coupla years. He does most of the pools on the street."

"I'll need his name." Diaz drew his small steno pad from his pants pocket.

"Ricky's Pool Service. I don't see him much. He's in and out in ten minutes, max."

"I need to ask you both to clear the area, but please don't leave the premises."

Walt wandered back into the guest house.

"Where's the cavalry?" Rex asked, reluctant to follow and miss out on the action.

"If you mean the cops, they're probably at Wendy's. I was on my way over when I got Walt's call." The detective scrutinized the body in the pool. "Another warning, I wonder?"

Just then, a lanky, fair-haired man in plain clothes stepped onto the patio through the sliding glass doors of the guest lounge. Rex recognized him as the cop who had followed Connie Lamont in a cab. He acknowledged Captain Diaz with a brief nod and then winced at the sight of the body in the pool. He, like Diaz, was in his mid to late thirties, no rookie, but possibly not yet inured to the death of a vibrant young person.

"Sergeant Pete Gallagher. Pete, this is Mr. Rex Graves, who takes an interest in solving murder cases."

"Awesome," Pete said. "Does that mean I can take the day off?" He winked at Rex, but his face showed tension and strain.

Two uniformed patrol officers joined them and greeted the detectives.

"No immediate sign of a purse or cell phone," Diaz told them. "Secure the perimeter and check the planters and foliage back there, and the alley. Lemme know soon as you find any I.D."

More barricade tape to adorn the bed-and-breakfast, Rex anticipated, feeling sorry for Walt who had been trying so hard to keep things running as smoothly as possible since his parents' death. "Let's step inside out of the way of the technicians," Diaz told Rex after exchanging a few words with the new arrivals.

Helen, dressed, and with lipstick applied, met them in the guest lounge. Ryan charged in after her, hair sticking up in all directions, as though he had just risen from bed, which was probably the case.

"Oh, man, this is insane," he exclaimed. "Walt said there's been a drowning?" He lunged at the glass slider, but Diaz held it shut.

"You can't go in there, son. Do you have any information that might help us?"

"Who is it?"

"We've yet to confirm. No one staying here. Where were you last night?"

Ryan took a moment to recall. "We were in the hot tub—me and my girlfriend. This was around ten. Then we went up to our room to shower before hitting the bars."

"I saw Ryan and Michelle leave," Rex confirmed. "Around eleven."

"We were out until about two," Ryan told Diaz. "And went straight up to bed."

"Sergeant Gallagher will take statements from everyone momentarily. In the meantime, please reallocate to the dining room." Diaz sent his sergeant to direct operations out front.

A crime scene investigator in a white zipper overall popped her hooded head around the glass slider and informed Captain Diaz that the gold bracelet on the victim's wrist bore an engraved name: Connie.

No other identification had been found.

# ~TWENTY-TWO~

"What is the connection between Connie Lamont and Merle and Taffy Dyer?" Rex asked the detective in the dining room, where Sergeant Pete Gallagher had corralled Walt and the guests.

The Barbers sat apart from the students, calmly eating a cold breakfast. Rex wondered if the sergeant had arranged the separation on purpose while he questioned Walt at Rex's usual table by the window. Michelle and Ryan nursed cans of soda. The girl's face was nude of makeup, her dark hair as bed-tangled as Ryan's.

"Wish I knew what the connection was," Diaz replied. "Like I said before, Ms. Lamont was uncooperative, to say the least. She was our best lead in the clown murders and now she's dead."

"Perhaps that's why."

Diaz shrugged his athletic shoulders. "She claimed she saw no one, but I didn't believe her.

She lied about being on the street, and yet a credible witness placed her there. Perhaps if she'd told us the truth, she wouldn't be in the pool."

"Willie said he was standing across the street and saw a black-bearded man force the Dyers into the kitchen at knifepoint."

"Willie, the bum?" Detective Diaz looked highly skeptical, as Rex predicted he would be.

"I was hoping to corroborate his story before I brought it to you."

"But Willie didn't see Connie?"

"Not that he mentioned to me. He might have come by way of Margaret Street, which leads direct to the cemetery. That's where I found him."

"Why did your black-bearded guy wait three days to kill Connie and run the risk of her talking?"

"Maybe she confronted him after the fact and tried to blackmail him."

"This all hangs on Willie's story." Diaz rubbed his smooth chin. "We could be going off on the wrong tangent entirely."

"The button was from the sleeve of Willie's coat."

"You sure? Stroke of luck you found it."

"I prefer to think of it as serendipity."

"I'll need to see his coat—"

"Here's the pool guy," Sergeant Gallagher announced to his superior, interrupting the conversation. "Richard Styles. He was cleaning the pool down the street."

He presented an emaciated individual who might have been buff in his prime, judging by the wasted muscles. Vestiges of chiseled good looks survived in his dissipated features beneath a mop of sun-bleached hair, streaked with gray. He wore a faded sleeveless T-shirt, long frayed khaki shorts, and rubber flip-flops. Rex noted, too, his large, work-roughened hands, tanned and weather-beaten like his face.

"You do the Dyers' pool?" Diaz asked the man.

"Every Wen-ez-day," he replied in a nasal drawl. Rex could detect cheap rum on his breath, even from where he stood a few feet away.

"Were you here earlier today?"

"Just got here. Started late on my route..."

"And was getting ready to turn his van around soon as he saw the patrol cars," Pete Gallagher supplied.

"Did you get a statement?" Diaz asked his sergeant.

"Yeah. Says he knows nuthin'."

"We may need to talk to you again later," Diaz told the pool man, dismissing him. "Your typical rummie Conch," he said as the individual limped from the room, followed by the sergeant. "No way Connie Lamont could've been overpowered by that guy. But I may want to take another look at him. He seems nervous."

"He's been drinking and driving," Rex suggested. And it wasn't even mid-morning yet.

Helen appeared with two mugs of coffee. "I remember from the Funky Parrot that you take yours black, Captain."

"Good memory!" Diaz took the mug from her hand. "This is very welcome, Helen. Thanks."

"Cream and sugar in yours," she said to Rex with a pointed smile, handing him his.

"I don't have to chase criminals down the street." He pointedly smiled at her in turn.

"We won't detain you longer than is necessary," Diaz addressed the room. "Your cooperation is much appreciated." He went to exchange a few words in private with Gallagher in the foyer.

"Poor woman," Helen said. "Strange her ending up in our pool."

"Horribly coincidental, you mean."

"Exactly. Please get to the bottom of this soon. I'm beginning to get the willies."

Diaz returned as Rex was helping himself to more coffee from the metal urn on the buffet table. The detective replenished his own mug.

"Pete got out of Walt Dyer that he was out last night until midnight, so he lied about being tucked up in bed. There's just something about that guy that doesn't add up. By all accounts, he resented his domineering parents. Perhaps something happened to push him over the edge. Maybe he likes killing things. Like those moths."

"And the cats."

"He admitted to killing the cats?"

Rex nodded gravely.

"He could be our black-bearded guy. Or else the black beard stuff is a load of b.s. dreamed up by our local friendly bum to score a hot meal."

"How did you know about the hot meal?"

"Pete followed you to the cemetery. We like to protect our tourists in Key West," Diaz said with a wide, white grin. "Our economy depends on you guys."

"Most kind," Rex said, a touch miffed that Captain Diaz had seen fit to keep tabs on him, and more so that he had not known he'd been followed. Clearly, he wasn't as clever as Connie Lamont, who had cottoned on to her tail and jumped into a taxi. All the same, he couldn't in all fairness hold the captain's actions against him. For all Diaz knew, the Scotsman could be a loose cannon jeopardizing an important criminal investigation. He hoped to set the record straight. And soon.

Diaz and Gallagher took Walt to a far corner of the room for further interviewing. Rex heard the chime of the front door, and Diane entered, flustered, and pale through her tan.

"What's with the new media circus outside?" she demanded. "What happened?" Then she saw her brother with the two detectives. "Are they gonna arrest him?" she asked Rex.

"Not sure. Have you not heard about the latest death?"

"I just got the kids off to school and snuck in before a reporter could... What do you mean by latest death?" The words died on Diane's anemic lips. "Are you serious? Who?" she asked in dread, looking around the dining room as though doing a head count.

"A woman. Not a guest at the Dolphin Inn."

"Who then? How?"

"A visitor to Key West. Strangled, possibly, and left in the pool. Or else she drowned."

"Our pool?"

"Diane, did you ever meet your ex-husband's girlfriend?"

"Tiffany? I never met her, exactly. I went to check her out one time at the sleazy club where she worked. Tiffany is her professional name, anyway, if that's what you call it," Diane said with distain.

"What does she look like?"

"Peroxide blonde, petite. That's her in the pool?"

"Apparently not. The victim doesn't fit your description. Just thought I'd try to rule out all possibilities." Including the far-fetched one where Diane lures her ex's girlfriend to her death. "Captain Diaz will be able to tell you more."

"Wish it was her. Wouldn't that be

something?" Diane's pinched face took on a pensive look. "A drowning. That might work for my novel."

Rex surmised there would be no lack of material for Diane's novel of vengeance. "I think we should probably deal with just the facts for now."

"Take him in," he heard Captain Diaz say.

Turning around, he saw the sergeant escort Walt toward the dining room door.

"I didn't do it!" Walt blubbered.

"You taking him to the police station?" Diane demanded.

"Just for further questioning. We're not gonna cuff him. He confessed to poisoning the cats," he told Rex as Walt left the bed-and-breakfast in Sergeant Gallagher's custody.

"What with?" Diane asked.

"Oleander. It's growing all over your yard."

"I never noticed. Why'd he do that? I've never known him do anything that cruel before."

First time for everything, Rex thought. Moths, cats—humans? Perhaps it showed an escalation.

"He was sending your parents an anonymous message, trying to get them to take early retirement," Diaz said.

"They should've listened."

Diaz drew Rex aside. "Perhaps he'll confess to the three murders under pressure. It's all circumstantial at this point, but what else we got?"

He cocked a thumb at the window. "Those vultures are circling for prey."

And Walt was being made the sacrificial lamb? Well, maybe the captain was right. Walt was the most likely suspect to-date in terms of means, motive, and opportunity.

"Plus he couldn't supply a good alibi for where he was last night," Captain Diaz added. "First he says he's in bed—same story as when his parents were murdered. But Ryan Ford and Michelle Cuzzens each stated in separate interviews that they heard him leave on his moped around ten-thirty. No one heard him come back. Then he says he can't say where he was, like he's protecting someone's reputation, like he's got a lady friend or boyfriend stashed somewhere. I'm thinking, married or underage? This dude is as kooky as those owls in the fireplace."

The charred iron birds stared out at them through amber orbs, watchful and eerie.

"Walt's reticence about what he was doing last night might have more to do with his actual whereabouts," Rex said. "Try House of the Rising Sun."

"You kidding me?" Diaz wrote a note in the steno pad, punctuating it with an emphatic question mark. "You his father confessor or what?"

"He says he used to work there and goes back to check on the girls from time to time. One of the girls' uncles told me Walt advanced her some money. I asked Walt aboot it."

Diaz flipped shut his pad. "You sure get around, Rex."

"I was *around* your police station when the biker uncle struck up a conversation with me. He heard me tell the desk sergeant I was there about the Dyer case. He had brought in a bag snatcher."

"Big dude, tatted up the arms?"

"Twisted Angel, I think he said his name was."

"That vigilante biker is Tom Halland, used to do stunts for TV and movies. Why couldn't Walt Dyer just come out and say he was paying a social call to some pros instead of wasting police time? I'm thinking can he be such a complete whack-job as he appears..."

"He was embarrassed you might get the wrong impression."

"He supposed right. It's hard to get a good impression of the guy. He acts guilty about everything." Diaz sighed and shook his head. "We'll check out his alibi and see if Walt Dyer is the charitable guy he makes himself out to be."

# ~TWENTY-THREE~

An hour passed. Rex glanced over at the Barbers who were industriously scribbling away on writing pads, Dennis beardless aside from his goatee, and weak-chinned, the physical opposite of any villain he could dream up for his novels. But still a more likely Blackbeard than Chuck Shumaker. Helen sat in a third chair, reading one of the books on the floral tablecloth. At a more remote table, the two students thumbed their Smartphones in desultory fashion.

"The M.E.'s opinion as to cause of death in this case is strangulation, like you said, and not drowning," Diaz informed Rex. He sat down beside him at the bay window, where the Scotsman sat watching the media vans parked on the street. Outside the front gate, reporters and cameramen lay in wait for potential interviewees from the guest house. "Déjà-vu all over again," as Helen had put it so aptly.

"Approximate time of death between midnight and three in the morning," the detective relayed. "Around the same time as the Dyers' deaths. Deep bruising around the neck consistent with the width of the scarf, plus petechial hemorrhaging in the conjunctiva. That's—"

"Red spots in the pink tissue around the eyeball caused by pressure erupting the tiny blood vessels," Rex interpreted. He had heard such testimony in court many times before, usually in cases of domestic violence.

"We'll know more after the autopsy," Captain Diaz said.

"Drowning someone would have made more noise. I imagine the killer met or brought her here, strangled her with her scarf, and carried her to the pool. That would take a fairly strong man or two people."

"Yup. Connie was tall and curvy. And there are no scuff marks on her stilettos or scrapes on her heels, so she wasn't dragged. We got a partial muddy print, hopefully the killer's. It was left on a page of a magazine by the pool."

That would be the magazine Diane had been reading, Rex recalled. "What sort of print?" he asked.

"Man's boot, medium size. Don't repeat any of this. It picked up dirt in the alley and must've stepped in water by the side of the pool—I'd guess from when the body splashed going in. Seems the boot's owner walked on the open magazine as he was leaving—print faces that way—not noticing it was there in the dark. Lucky break for us."

The pool man was wearing flip-flops and, in any case, he didn't look strong enough to carry a woman of Connie's stature, Rex reasoned. And he had only ever seen Walt in loafers.

"Michelle Cuzzens is set to inherit a million bucks. That's a powerful motive for two kids starting out," Diaz remarked, looking in their direction, specifically at Ryan's feet. The student wore leather sandals. "And a sum worth protecting from someone who might know something about the Dyers' murders."

Michelle and Ryan rested their heads in their arms on the table, tired or bored, and possibly hung over. They had all been in the dining room for hours while law enforcement busied themselves outside.

"Would Connie Lamont agree to meet a dangerous stranger in a dark alley?" Rex queried.

Diaz shrugged his shoulders, seemingly at a loss. "Those kids are at school in Florida. She lived in Fort Lauderdale. That's Ryan Ford's home town."

"And she came to Key West alone. Why?"

"We scanned her prints into the NCIC

database after she obligingly drank from a glass of water she was offered at the police station. No priors. Never been married, no kids, never—"

"Never married," Rex repeated thoughtfully. "Maybe she was looking for a partner. An attractive woman in her mid-thirties..."

"Internet dating," Helen suggested, joining their table and perching on a chair. "Looking for a tall, dark, handsome stranger?"

"We're still working our way through all the hotels, motels, apartment rentals, and B and B's, but she could have been staying at a friend's." Diaz sighed in frustration.

"Try the Banyan Inn on Frances Street," Helen said all of a sudden. The two men turned on her. "Mike, he said his name was. Tall, broad shoulders, black beard, blue eyes. He's the owner. He was among the crowd that first morning watching what was going on," she explained.

"Revisiting the scene," Rex speculated. "I wonder. I thought at the time he seemed to know a lot aboot the Dyers, from what you told me. I never met him," he informed Diaz.

"I know Cap'n Mike," Diaz said.

"Not my type, though. Too dangerous by half, but a lot of women go for that sort." Helen gave a small shrug. "Not sure what made me think of him just then. I suppose it was the tall, dark, handsome part."

"Perhaps that's why Connie Lamont didn't

come forward," Rex said, pursuing his own train of thought. "Perhaps she was protecting him."

"Mike Free fits our profile for the murders," Diaz agreed. "He's strong, and those knots in the double homicide would have been a cinch for a boat captain. And he's dangerous, alright. I've had a few run-ins with him in my time."

Peggy Barber, who had been following the latter part of the conversation, remarked that Helen's description of Mike Free matched her memory of the visitor to the guest house two years ago, the man she had seen again in the crowd outside Charlie's Restaurant. "Oh, don't you remember, Den? He would be perfect to play our hero."

Dennis professed not to recall such a character, insisting he hadn't been present when the man in question came to the Dolphin Inn looking for Taffy Dyer. "Who would remember a minor incident from two years ago?" he asked helplessly.

"I would," Peggy responded. "He was quite striking."

"My parents told everybody who would listen that Mike Free was a drug smuggler," Diane informed the room from where she stood at the window, observing the action on the street. "I never met him, but I'll bet he's Blackbeard."

"Blackbeard?" Captain Diaz asked, furrowing his smooth brow.

"My mother's 'friend,'" Diane replied,

wrapping quotation marks around the word with her fingers. "I thought she was making him up."

"Unfortunately, the smuggling was never proved," Diaz said. "He was charged but never convicted. I remember he sold his boat and used the proceeds from that and possibly his ill-gotten gains to purchase the Banyan Inn. It had fallen into disrepair and he picked it up cheap."

"He stole a lot of business from my parents, or so they said. Taffy must've gotten under his skin big-time. She can't have known what she was dealing with."

"A cool-under-fire character, if ever I met one," Diaz recalled. "Guess you'd have to be, dodging hurricanes at sea, not to mention Columbian pirates and the U.S. Coast Guard. And then evading the IRS. But I never pegged him for a cold-blooded killer. Wish we coulda sent him down with the other smugglers, but he had a girlfriend swear blind he was holed up with her."

"He's a lady's man," Helen said. "He was giving me the eye and asking how long I'd be in town. I told him I had disembarked in Key West for the day, off a cruise to Mexico. I'm sure he wouldn't have been so chatty if he knew I'd be staying in town and my fiancé was a famous solver of murder crimes."

"Och, I'm not famous."

"Whoa, guys," Diaz intervened. "It's a long shot, but I'll send one of my men over to the

Banyan and check it out. Problem is, we don't have probable cause to search his place. Just because Helen saw him in a crowd of onlookers Sunday morning..."

"What if Taffy Dyer was blackmailing him?" Rex thought for a moment. "Merle might not have known about his wife's arrangement with Free that was keeping her in drink she could not otherwise afford, but he probably knew about Captain Mike's nefarious activities past and, possibly, present."

"That makes sense," Diane said. "Why else would he give her booze? That's just like Taffy—badmouthing everybody. He put the bag over her head to shut her up. And Merle too."

"And then he silenced Connie Lamont," Rex added. "And dumped her in the pool to frame Walt Dyer, the obvious suspect in his parents' murders."

"And a known weirdo." Diane shrugged her skinny shoulders in the gray denim sundress. "Yeah, I know he's my brother, but it's the truth. What he went through as a kid wasn't natural. Taffy totally screwed us up."

Helen put a comforting arm around Diane's shoulders. Captain Diaz meanwhile was listening, watching, and obviously thinking. He finally spoke.

"There might be something to the blackmailing theory." He pulled his pad from his pocket and flipped back through the pages until he found what he was looking for. "This is a transcript from a note written on Taffy Dyer's PC. It was deleted, but our computer expert was able to recover it from the hard drive. 'Hi, there, Night Hawk,' " Diaz read. " 'Following up on my letter—do we have a deal? You have much to lose. Taffy.' " The detective looked up for reactions from Diane and Rex.

"Is Night Hawk the same person as Blackbeard?" Diane asked.

Diaz lifted his shoulders, implying he had no idea. "The name or moniker doesn't come up anywhere else on her computer. The note is dated a month ago. It doesn't say much in and of itself, and our IT guy wasn't able to retrieve the original letter referred to in the note. Could be a legitimate business transaction, but the tone is less than cordial."

"Night Hawk could be Blackbeard," Diane persisted. "Is it enough to go after Mike Free?"

Mouth askew in his clean-shaven face, Diaz seemed to weigh his options. "We have nothing to pin Connie's murder on him. If I question him, he'll lawyer up like he did before. He has a sleazy attorney out of Miami who specializes in drug-related arrests and got Free off the hook when we had more evidence than we have now. If I can prove some tangible connection with Connie Lamont, we might have something. But we don't know if she stayed at the Banyan and, if she did, whether any evidence or witnesses can be found attesting to that fact. If he's responsible for her death, he'll probably deny knowing her. He might take off. A single man with a struggling B and B and a knowledge of boats and places to hide out is a big flight risk."

"If we go posing as prospective guests, we might find a link between him and Connie Lamont," Rex said. "He introduced himself to Helen and told her about the Banyan Inn, so it would seem natural enough if we went over to enquire aboot alternative accommodation in light of this latest murder."

"Don't know that *I* want to stay on here," Diane exclaimed. "But I guess I'll have to while Walt is tied up at the station. When are you gonna release him?"

Peggy Barber chimed in with the comment that they too would check out if they weren't already due to leave the next day. Would the cops provide security at the Dolphin Inn? she inquired. Michelle seconded the request from across the room.

Diaz assured them he would see what he could do. "I may have a better idea than you posing as prospective guests at the Banyan Inn," he told Rex and Helen. "If Mike Free has been hanging around here keeping his eyes and ears open, he may have heard that you're investigating the murders."

"Then what do you have in mind?" Rex asked.

"How about a little Fantasy Fest disguise?" Diaz grinned at him. "Perhaps spook him into some sort of admission that he knew Connie."

## ~TWENTY-FOUR~

"Helen, you look ravishing as a brunette," Rex said.

"Just support my arm, please, before I break my neck in these bloody stilettos."

She wore large Jackie O sunglasses, which didn't look out of place in the Florida sunshine, though the red lipstick was a bit extreme for Helen, who typically favored a pale shade of pink. The long dark wig and red scarf completed the transformation.

They had alighted from the pink flamingo taxicab at a corner of Frances, lavishly tipping the driver who swore he had seen his female fare before. "A dead ringer," he had insisted, almost salivating. A most unsavory fellow, Rex thought, regretting his tip, but not wanting to wait around for change. Important business beckoned.

A sudden steamy shower that morning had

quickly burned off on the pavement, doing little to alleviate the cloying midday air.

Helen sashayed precariously along the sidewalk, the long scarf, which shopping maven Rosa had supplied along with her other clothes, floating in the humid breeze. "It's not a perfect disguise," Helen allowed. "Connie was much taller, but hopefully it'll give our suspect a jolt."

The idea of Rex wearing a wire had been entertained and dismissed, not least because the subtropical climate precluded easy concealment of such a device in one's clothes. However, the cell phone that Captain Diaz had loaned him might conceivably record something if he got the opportunity.

Diaz had reported to Rex that police inquiries made among Key West's preeminent innkeepers or, at least, those most active in their professional association, had unearthed rumors about Mike Free's drug-smuggling past, which the Dyers had done all they could to keep alive. "Cap'n Mike," according to most, had abandoned his illegal activities and was an upstanding member of the community. Taffy, on the other hand, had entertained illusions of grandeur and grated on everyone's nerves.

The Dyers had complained about the state of the Banyan property. The other innkeepers claimed there was nothing that a lick of paint and a slap of wood treatment couldn't put right.

However, the Dyers, and Taffy especially, had suggested that Free's place of business posed health and safety hazards, and spared no energy or restraint warning their guests who might be lured by his cheaper rates. This had been substantiated by Raphael Ramirez, who had approached other bed-and-breakfasts looking for a job after being fired from the Dolphin Inn. He had not resurfaced in spite of the police using their best efforts to locate him. One source had suggested he had drifted to Miami.

In short, the innkeepers appeared to be on Free's side, and Diaz feared word of his inquiries would get back to his suspect. Time was of the essence.

Rex hoped the charade he and Helen planned did not turn into a farce. None of the innkeepers had been able or willing to identify Night Hawk. All Rex and the KWPD had against Mike Free was his dark beard, some nifty nautical knots, and possible blackmail.

The couple paused outside the Banyan Inn named for the huge tree in the front yard. Buttressed by lesser trunks packed as tightly as organ pipes, the tree planed above the roof of the board-and-batten building. A rope hammock swung between a pair of sapodilla trees. Yellowed crotons and silver buttonwood crammed the shrubbery beds on either side of sun-bleached wooden steps leading to a porch fronting the guest house. Its shaded and secluded setting among the shimmering gumbo-limbo, key lime, and palmetto trees recently sprinkled by rain would obscure the street from the green-shuttered windows downstairs. Rex hoped for the element of surprise.

"I'll go in first, make sure he's there." He preceded Helen up the warped porch steps. They were in luck. A man with a trimmed black beard, mid to late forties, was in conversation with a youngish woman wearing a fruit-patterned apron. He turned to face Rex squarely as the door chime sounded.

The foyer felt refreshingly cool after the full impact of the sun on the street. "Are you the proprietor?"

"That's me," the man answered, a devil-may-care twinkle in his ocean blue eyes.

Rex, holding the front door open, signaled to Helen, who stepped through the gap and met Mike Free's amazed, slack-jawed stare.

"Connie," the woman in the apron began with hesitation in her voice. Pasty-faced beneath a cascade of coppery curls, she peered nearsightedly at the apparition in the scarlet scarf and stilettos. "Did you leave something in room?" she asked in an Eastern European accent. "I thought you checked out already."

"Shut up, Katya," Free growled. "It's not Connie."

"That's right," Rex told him. "Connie Lamont is dead."

Free did not flinch. He nonchalantly rolled back the sleeves on his blue linen shirt, exposing strong, darkly matted forearms. "I don't know what you're talking about," he drawled.

"Apparently you knew Connie well enough to realize this is not the same woman, so that's a start. You remember my fiancée Helen from outside the Dolphin Inn Sunday morning?"

Helen removed her wig and sunglasses.

"Hey, doll," Free said with a provocative wink.

Rex resisted the urge to deck him in his bearded jaw, but mostly because he did not fancy his chances, in spite of his superior height and bulk.

"What's with the disguise?"

"What was your relationship with Connie Lamont?" Rex questioned.

"What's yours?"

"I asked first."

"I didn't have 'a relationship.' "

"Katya," Rex said, with all the Scottish charm he could muster. "I'm sure you have a guest book. They seem to be a prerequisite in bed-and-breakfast establishments."

The young woman's face—she could not have been more than thirty-five in Rex's estimation—showed incomprehension. She glanced at Mike, who shrugged his broad shoulders, reverting his insistent blue gaze at Helen, who began to blush under the scrutiny. The phrase "salty dog" sprang to Rex's mind. No wonder Peggy Barber had associated him with her pirate hero. He attributed his impression to the short beard threaded with silver, the careless sweep of dark hair across the tanned and furrowed brow, and the lean-packed body straining against the button-down shirt tucked in his jeans; but most of all it was the insolent blue, womanizing eyes. Rex guessed he might be staring at Helen to unnerve him, and he refused to take the bait. If it did come to a fight, he'd be the one to end up flat on his back on the polished wood floor, knocked out as cold as the antique scroll-work boot scraper by the front door. This drew Rex's attention to what Free was wearing on his feet: a pair of trainers.

Katya brought Rex the guest book, a ring-binder with a laminated cover depicting palm trees and striped umbrellas on a sugar sand beach. Rex examined the entries, working back to the previous week, where a line had been whited out, but not sufficiently to disguise a couple of letters which could have spelled Connie Lamont.

"Were you waiting for it to dry before writing over it?" he asked Katya, who appeared to be reacting more strongly to Free's attentions to Helen than Rex was.

"Not me. Him," she said sullenly, regarding the innkeeper with defiance.

"So what if the lady was a guest here? What business is it of yours?"

"Just a guest?"

Free encircled the woman's waist. "Ask Katya, my housekeeper and future wife."

Katya swung out of his grasp and slapped his face. "Get your filthy hands off me! I find your condom wrappers in her room!"

Ah-ha, thought Rex triumphantly. Unfortunately, chlorinated water would have eliminated any of Free's DNA on the pool victim.

"And now you make bedroom eyes at this blonde!"

Mike Free spun on Katya. "Have you done Ms. Lamont's room yet?"

"Don't bother changing the sheets, lass," Rex told her. "The police will want to take a close look." Hopefully, not all traces of Free could be erased as easily as Connie's name in the register.

The wail and yelp of approaching sirens had the effect of propelling Mike Free toward the front door, practically knocking Helen off her feet in the process. Rex ran out onto the porch in time to see the innkeeper take off on a Steve McQueen-style motorbike parked at the curb, and cut in between two patrol cars blocking the Fleming Street intersection, roof lights flashing. Rex knew Diaz was with his sergeant in an unmarked vehicle positioned somewhere strategic to the proceedings, perhaps in the red Dodge

Charger with the heavily tinted windows parked among the other cars on the street. As the matte black motorbike sped away in a throaty snarl, the cop cars executed a U-turn and gave chase.

Rex watched helplessly as Mike Free tried to make his escape.

## ~TWENTY-FIVE~

Rex darted back into the lobby.

"Katya," he asked the woman standing beside Helen and wringing her hands on her apron. "Where would he go? You must tell me. He in all probability murdered Connie Lamont. Don't make yourself an accomplice."

"Why he kill her?"

"I believe she saw him murder the owners of the Dolphin Inn."

Katya's pale globular eyes widened. "He hated the Dyers. Big, big hate." She swept her arms in an arc. "They lost him much business. They gossip about him, call him drug dealer. Connie, I find out from doing her room, came from Fort Lauderdale to be with him. He try to keep it secret from me! But I find folder with his picture and emails. She follow him at night. I see her go out when he leaves."

233

"Where would he go now?"

"His fishing boat."

"I thought he'd sold it."

"A smaller boat, *Night Hawk*, he keeps at Garrison Bight. Sailing is in his blood. Never would he be without boat."

Rex ran out of the guest house holding the recording cell phone. He speed-dialed Captain Diaz. Unbelievably, he was directed to the detective's voice mail. He relayed Katya's information as succinctly as possible, cursing as he ended the call. Diaz must be on his radio or else on a more important call. At that moment, the thunderous roar of motorcycle engines approached from the north end of Frances, the direction Free had taken. He spotted a red bandanna on one biker, a round helmet on the other, and flagged them down. Twisted Angel grinned at him beneath a pair of aviator sunglasses and, swerving at the last minute in a blaze of chrome, skidded to a stop. His leather booted foot hit the blacktop. Rollin' Roy pulled up beside him.

"Can I cadge a lift?" Rex shouted over the revved throttles.

"Where you going?" Twisted asked.

"Garrison Bight. I'm chasing a man wanted by the police."

"That's where we're headed. Hop on."

As they took off, he heard Helen call after him.

He turned and waved briefly, preferring to hold onto Twisted Angel's midsection with both hands for safety. He did not have time to register her expression, but had no difficulty imagining it. They tore back up Frances onto Eaton and looped onto the Palm Avenue Causeway, crossing the bridge bisecting the inlet, all at terrifying and illegal speed, and caught up with the wailing police cars with their lights going berserk. Twisted Angel overtook them, weaving between the traffic that was attempting to get out of the way of the cops.

The warm breeze ruffled Rex's hair and inflated his short sleeve cotton shirt as the scenery streaked by, aquamarine sea and watercraft on one side; concrete strip malls on the other.

"Where to now?" Twisted Angel yelled over his shoulder after turning the Harley into the marina, Rollin' Roy on their tail.

"Mike Free's boat," Rex shouted in his ear. "*Night Hawk*. You know it?"

"Charter Boat Row."

Houseboats lined the dock, two and three-level structures on floating platforms attached to land by wooden gangways. The water trailer park displayed an array of colors, exterior wall ornaments with a nautical theme, and window boxes planted with flowers. Other house boats rebelled against such bohemian aesthetics, storing rusted bikes, crates, and coils of rope on their railed-in decks, while flotsam and jetsam rode the metallic gray ripples below.

A tang of diesel, fresh paint, and low tide assailed Rex's nose as Twisted Angel navigated the bike under the bridge and sped toward a line of charter boats advertising under the names of their captains emblazoned on large signs. Mike Free's was not among them but, as they pulled up to the new wood dock, Rex spotted him leap onto one of the boats, *Night Hawk*, while a second man cast off the ropes amid a roar of engines and a surge of pungent fumes. The sturdy thirty-footer, equipped with a tuna tower atop a weathered wheelhouse, looked as though it had braved the elements on many occasions. Seagulls swooped and cried raucously in the vessel's wake. Free had escaped once again.

Rex dismounted from the motorcycle and, while the bikers compared notes on the breakneck ride, he tried Diaz's cell phone again, and this time got his live voice.

"I'm at Garrison Bight Marina at Charter Boat Row. Mike Free just boarded the *Night Hawk* and he's getting away!" Twisted Angel had run every light and broken every speed limit, and still they hadn't managed to stop Mike Free. Rex had entertained a fantasy of the Hells Angel wrestling Free to the ground and giving him a dunking in the oily water. "Your patrol cars got stuck in traffic," he informed Diaz. "Wait, I think I hear them." Not that they could do anything unless they were amphibious.

"Don't sweat it, Rex," the captain said, all calm and coolness on the phone, his voice not rising one octave. "We got police boats. We'll send out a chopper if we have to. *Night Hawk*, huh? Taffy Dyer must have known about the boat. By the way, how'd you get there so fast?"

"You don't want to know."

Diaz chuckled. "No tickets, I promise. Stay right there until we arrive. You did great."

Right now *Night Hawk* would be winging her way toward the mouth of the bight. "Ah, well," Rex told Angel, punching his massive bicep in admiration of his motorcycling feats. "At least we know where he's headed."

"Yeah, somewhere into the Gulf." Seated on the motorcycle, the biker looked as dispirited as Rex felt.

# ~TWENTY-SIX~

"I can't believe you just took off like that," Helen remonstrated after Twisted Angel had dropped Rex back off at the Dolphin Inn. This followed a couple or more beers aboard the Hells Angels' psychedelic houseboat, where an assortment of Harley Davidson paraphernalia served as decoration befitting the mildewed shag carpet and retro furnishings. Rex had been unable to decide if the décor was meant to look retro or if, in fact, it was.

"I had no choice but to take off," he told her. "And it's just as well I did. The police were too slow. I couldn't afford to lose Mike Free. He could have sailed away to South America."

"You weren't even wearing a helmet."

"It's not required by law here in the States."

"That's crazy. You're required to wear a seatbelt in a car."

"I felt quite safe in Angel's hands. In fact, it was the ride of my life." Rex, under the anesthetizing effect of a few beers, had all but forgotten his terror on the loudly reverberating machine weaving and tearing along at breakneck speed.

The effort to remain serious failed Helen, and she laughed. "Hardly a good example to set your son."

"I won't tell him if you won't. I think he prefers to think of me as a stodgy old fuddy-duddy."

"Come here, old Fuddy-Duddy, while I give you a kiss and show you how worried I've been about you."

The embrace was curtailed by the urgent ring of the cell phone in Rex's pocket. He wandered out onto the balcony where the jasmine was beginning to sweeten the warm air and re-entered the bedroom some fifteen minutes later, beaming as broadly as his mouth would allow. "That was Dan Diaz. He's invited us round to his house for dinner tomorrow."

"You were on the phone for ages. It must have been about more than a dinner invitation. Plus, you're grinning all over your face. Oh, Rex, can it be you have a soft crush on our charming Captain Diaz?"

"A soft... What on earth do you mean?"

"I detect a sort of schoolboy infatuation..."

Rex pondered this surprising observation. "I like the man, that's all. He's personable and straightforward. And okay, I admire him. He never seems to get rattled."

"That's all I meant. I think the term now is bro-mance. I think it's rather sweet."

"Nonsense. Can we move on?" Rex asked, feeling uncomfortable. "There is more important news. Free has been apprehended offshore. The boat's been impounded. It's registered in the name of a mate of Free's who is doing time for smuggling."

"Well, that's certainly cause for celebration. Did the police find anything onboard?"

"Aye, traces of contraband in a false compartment in the hull. They also found a computer-generated letter blackmailing Mike Free and signed 'TD' in typeface. If that's Taffy Dyer, she was threatening to expose his new smuggling activities to Drug Enforcement. Seems like what she and Merle were saying aboot him was true, and he didn't like it."

"Enough to murder them both in cold blood."

"Diaz obtained warrants for the first degree murders of the Dyers and hopes to get Free to confess to Ms. Lamont's." Rex paced the room, hands in his pockets. "Free apparently seized the opportunity of Fantasy Fest to suffocate the Dyers in their kitchen, hoping to implicate the son and generally confuse the police by adding the guests and any number of bacchanalians to the suspect pool."

"His plan might have worked, but for Connie."

Rex extracted his pipe from his pocket in preparation for a leisurely puff on the balcony watching the doves in the Poinciana trees. "Unfortunately for our lady in the red scarf, she witnessed more than she bargained for. Diaz's team found a possible match for the boot print by the pool when searching Free's closet at the Banyan Inn. It's the connecting piece of evidence they need. Plus, the blue linen shirt he was wearing when apprehended has faint striations in the sleeves. Seems Connie might've clawed at his arms when he was strangling her."

The poor woman had struggled for her life. She had come to Key West looking for love and had found death. With any luck, the crime lab would identify microscopic red polish chippings in the material as a final nail in Free's coffin.

"It does not look as though he'll escape justice this time around," he assured his fiancée, who had shuddered at the mention of Connie attempting to defend herself from her assailant.

"So, what happens now?" Helen asked. "Can you finally relax and start calling this a real holiday?"

"I intend to. I should call Campbell and finalize arrangements for his trip. He left a message with Walt to say Melodie was coming too. Dan Diaz has granted me full use of this phone for the duration of our stay, courtesy of the Key West Police Department. After that and a smoke, I'm all yours until dinner."

"Promises, promises," Helen said with a flirtatious smile.

## ~TWENTY-SEVEN~

Rex and Helen picked Campbell and his girlfriend up from Key West International Airport, seven minutes' drive away from the Dolphin Inn, and brought them back in the cab. To Walt's gratification, Rex had reserved the Poet's Attic. All but the students had left.

"I'm a poet and I know it," Campbell quipped, dumping his bag on one of the twin brass beds tucked beneath the skylight. A paperback tumbled out of a canvas pocket, the posthumously published *Islands in the Stream* by Ernest Hemingway.

"Any good?" Rex asked.

"I like it so far. The islands in the Stream are Key West, Cuba, and Bimini, Hemingway's favorite fishing spots." Campbell had always loved to fish. "I thought it would make for appropriate reading on the trip."

He had grown out his blond curls and sideburns, which accentuated the delicate angles of his face. He looked a lot like his mother, Rex reminisced with a tug in his heart.

"This is so adorable," Melodie said, her sweep of caramel-colored hair shimmering in the lamplight. The sloping ceiling was papered with bouquets of forget-me-nots on a cream background, the few sticks of knotted pine furniture lending a rustic charm to the room.

"Scarcely big enough to swing a cat," Campbell joked, bumping his head on a beam. "Ow."

"Enough with the cats," Rex said, recalling Macavity and his less fortunate fellow felines. "And you're next door to the students, Ryan and Michelle."

"Par-*tay!*" Campbell trumpeted.

"A weekend in Key West! I can't believe it," Mel exclaimed. "Thank you." Her remarkable violet eyes shone with emotion as she gave Rex a big hug.

He had grown extremely fond of the girl since he solved the tragic case of her brother's alleged suicide at Hilliard University in Jacksonville. She and his son had formed a bond during that distressing time, and Campbell had all but been adopted by the Clark family, where he had become a surrogate son. Their staying at the Dolphin Inn had been Campbell's idea. He had allayed his father's concerns that the murders might affect her. The circumstances of her brother's death were so different, and it had been over three years since it happened. Notwithstanding, Rex had spoken to Walt and Diane, and no one was to bring up the recent events in Melodie's presence, even though she knew the basic facts.

"I'm glad of the chance to see you both again before the spring," he told the young couple, who were due to visit for his and Helen's wedding.

Rex predicted other wedding bells in the not-too-distant future, but he hoped to have a breathing space in between. Dennis Barber had pointed out how grueling and expensive weddings could be. The Barbers had departed for Kansas, and the four of them had promised to keep in touch. Rex had filled in the Shumakers in Dayton about developments in the case, as promised. Hearing about the third murder, Chuck had joked on the phone, "So, Rex, you unmasked the serial cereal killer!"

"Why don't you both get freshened up and we'll go out for dinner?" Rex suggested to Campbell and Melodie before rejoining Helen in their room.

Half an hour later, as the two couples approached Sloppy Joe's Bar, a thunderous swarm of bikers in motley gear led by Twisted Angel slowed down and, extending muscle-bound arms in unison gave Rex a thumbs-up salute. Rex waved back enthusiastically. A fitting finale to the case, he thought with intense satisfaction.

"What was all that about?" Campbell asked, staring at the chromed rear ends of the receding Harleys.

"Friends of your dad's," Helen explained.

"You got in with a gang of Hells Angels?" Campbell shook his head in disbelief. "Yeah, right."

"You make them sound like a band of highway robbers."

"I don't get it. How do you know them?"

"It's a long story."

Campbell, almost as tall as his father, clapped him on the shoulder. "You can take as long as you like over a couple of beers. And you never did explain how you figured out who murdered the people at the Dolphin Inn."

"I want to hear too," Melodie insisted.

"Rex found out that the killer had a black beard, and he also pieced together the blackmailing theory," Helen said.

"But you clinched it by remembering Mike Free," Rex countered.

"We make a good team."

They kissed.

"Oh, my word," Campbell said, rolling his eyes. "I think I'm going into sugar shock. Seriously, though, I'm glad he got caught before he could do more harm."

"Thanks to you guys," Melodie added. "But wasn't it all incredibly scary? I mean, wouldn't you rather have gone on your cruise to Mexico?"

Helen smiled brightly at Rex. "Not on your life!"

Rex had to wonder—had Helen caught the murder-solving bug?

REX'S ENTRY IN THE DOLPHIN INN GUEST
BOOK:

"Wonderful hospitality is to be had at the Dolphin Inn where the capable new proprietors, Diane and Walt Dyer, provide a delectable breakfast in comfortable and cheery surroundings located close to the main tourist attractions. If ever we return to Key West, this is where we'll stay once again. Highest recommendation."

Signed *Rex Graves, QC*, Edinburgh, Scotland

OTHER BOOKS IN THE REX GRAVES MYSTERY
SERIES:

# *Christmas Is Murder*

## *Starred* Review from *Booklist:*

The first installment in this new mystery series is a
winner. The amateur detective is Rex Graves, a
Scottish barrister, fond of Sudoku puzzles and Latin
quotations. In an old-fashioned conceit, Challinor begins
with a cast of characters, along with hints of possible
motives for each. Although set firmly in the present, this
tale reads like a classic country-house mystery. Rex
and the others are snowed in at the Swanmere Manor
hotel in East Sussex, England. Being the last to arrive,
Rex immediately hears of the unexpected demise of
one of the other guests. By the time the police arrive
days later, additional bodies have piled up and motives
are rampant, but Rex has identified the murderer. At
times, it seems we are playing Clue or perhaps enjoying
a contemporary retelling of a classic Agatha Christie
tale *(And Then There Were None,* or *At Bertram's
Hotel)* with a charming new sleuth. A must for cozy
fans.

# Murder in the Raw

### Mystery Scene Magazine:

In *Murder in the Raw*, Scottish barrister Rex Graves must expose—and I do mean expose—the killer of Sabine Durand, a French actress who goes missing one evening from a nudist resort in the Caribbean... Set on an island, *Murder in the Raw* is a clever variant on the locked room mystery, and Rex discovers that everyone in this self-contained locale has a secret when it comes to the intriguing Sabine. Who, though, would benefit from her disappearance or murder? With a host of colorful characters, a dose of humor and a balmy locale, you will want to devour this well-plotted mystery. I won't spoil your pleasure by divulging the solution, but suffice it to say that Challinor provides a most compelling answer.

# Phi Beta Murder*

## Foreword Magazine:

Readers meet up once again with Rex Graves in the third mystery to follow the Scottish barrister with a knack for getting involved in the ultimate crime. Rex is on his way out of the beautiful Scottish countryside leaving behind Helen, his new woman friend and his mother to visit his son on the campus of his American college. Campbell Graves is supposed to be enjoying life at Hilliard University in Jacksonville, Florida, but lately on the phone he's sounded rather distant, and Rex wants nothing more than to see his son and make sure everything is all right. Unfortunately the day he steps on campus is the day a young man is found in his locked room hanging from the ceiling. Soon Rex must split his time between worrying about his son, solving a crime that seems to involve a million people with a million different agendas, and trying to balance his love life without losing people in the process. Humor and well-written characters add to the story, as does some reflection on the causes of suicide. A wonderful read and great plot for cozy mystery lovers.

* *This title has not been endorsed by the Phi Beta Kappa Society. The Phi Beta Kappa fraternity depicted in the novel is in no way affiliated nor associated with the Phi Beta Kappa Society.*

251

# Murder on the Moor

**BellaOnline:**

Scottish Barrister and amateur sleuth Rex Graves purchased Gleneagle Lodge so that he and his girlfriend, Helen D'Arcy, could get away to spend some private time together. Now he wonders why he had agreed to host a housewarming party. When one of the guests turns up dead, her body found in a nearby loch, the finger-pointing begins. Graves cannot help but put his sleuthing skills to work as he tries to find out who killed his house guest while he also gathers clues as to who is committing the so-called Moor Murders. He is wondering if the two are tied and if he is hosting the killer. When a storm prevents anyone from leaving, Rex and Helen do their best to keep everyone calm during their forced confinement. Set in the Scottish Highlands, Challinor successfully utilizes the atmosphere of the countryside to enhance the tension going on inside the Lodge. The characters seem typical of the type seen in many mysteries written by such authors as Agatha Christie, and are a welcome diversion from today's style of writing. The writing is crisp and the story fast-paced. The inevitable gathering of the guests in the library comes with a twist or two, and the ending is a satisfying conclusion to a solid whodunit.

# Murder of the Bride

## *Buried Under Books:*

Rex Graves is back, this time visiting his fiancée, Helen d'Arcy, so they can attend the wedding in Aston-on-Trent of one of her former students. Polly Newcombe is very pregnant and her groom, Timmy Thorpe looks a bit peaked, but is it just the dreary day leading Rex to think the success of this marriage is doubtful? Perhaps not, as the reception at the bride's family country home in Derbyshire soon turns from a pleasant celebration to a scene of mayhem when Polly collapses, looking more than a little green. Leaving the reception and heading to Aston-on-Trent, Rex learns a great deal more about the secrets of the Newcombe and Thorpe families. Is jealousy behind the attacks? Greed? Infidelity? Overbearing mothers? Rex and the local police have an overabundance of clues and evidence, and getting to the solution to the case will require much thought and cooperation. This latest case for Rex Graves is every bit as charming and entertaining as those in earlier books and readers will not be disappointed. The setting, an English country home, is as much a character as the people, and many of those characters are a delight, especially Police Constable Perrin (and the cast of characters provided by the author is very much appreciated).

# ABOUT THE AUTHOR

C.S. Challinor was born in Bloomington, Indiana, and was educated in Scotland and England. She now lives in Southwest Florida.

All Rex Graves titles (one through five published by Midnight Ink Books) are available in trade paperback, Kindle, Nook, etc. *Christmas Is Murder*, the first in the series, is also available in LP hardcover (Thorndike Reviewer's Choice). *Murder of the Bride* was selected as a Mystery Guild Book Club pick (hardcover).

*STANDALONE TITLES:*

*Breathtaking*, a romantic mystery set in Southwest Florida and Kauai, featuring real estate agent, Angelica Lane.

Visit the author at *www.rexgraves.com*.

CPSIA information can be obtained at www.ICGtesting.com
Printed in the USA
LVOW101320130513

333533LV00009B/44/P